Coretta Scott King

D0094299

Illustrated by
Meryl Henderson

Coretta Scott King

FIRST LADY OF CIVIL RIGHTS

by George E. Stanley

ALADDIN PAPERBACKS
New York London Toronto Sydney

❧

ALADDIN PAPERBACKS
An imprint of Simon & Schuster Children's Publishing Division
1230 Avenue of the Americas, New York, NY 10020
Text copyright © 2008 by George E. Stanley
Illustrations copyright © 2008 by Meryl Henderson
All rights reserved, including the right of reproduction
in whole or in part in any form.
ALADDIN PAPERBACKS and related logo and CHILDHOOD OF FAMOUS
AMERICANS are registered trademarks of Simon & Schuster, Inc.
Designed by Chris Grassi
The text of this book was set in New Caledonia.
Manufactured in the United States of America
First Aladdin Paperbacks edition December 2008
2 4 6 8 10 9 7 5 3 1
Library of Congress Control Number 2008932193
ISBN-13: 978-1-4169-6800-9
ISBN-10: 1-4169-6800-8

ILLUSTRATIONS

CONTENTS

Coretta Scott King

Dreamer

April 27, 1927, was warm for late spring in Alabama. Some of the church ladies who had come to the Scott farmhouse were using anything they could find to fan themselves as they waited to be told if their help was needed to keep Mrs. Scott comfortable while the baby was waiting to be born.

"Don't go in there, Edythe, honey," Mrs. Franklin said. "Your mama can't visit with you now, child."

Two-year-old Edythe Scott stuck out her

lower lip, looked for a minute as though she was going to cry, and then left the room.

"It's always hard on the first child when a new one comes along," Mrs. Johnston said. "All of a sudden, they're no longer the center of everyone's attention."

"Oh, you don't have to worry about Edythe," Mrs. Holden said. "Bernice and Obie have enough love in their hearts for lots of children."

Mrs. Franklin waved a hand around the room where they were sitting. "The Good Lord has blessed them with material things, too, that most of us don't have," she said, "but they never act as though they're better than the rest of us."

Mrs. Johnson snorted. "I think the word you're looking for, Sister Franklin, is 'uppity,'" she said. She shook her head. "No, I don't think any white folks would describe the Scotts as 'uppity.'"

Obadiah Scott, whom everyone called Obie,

had built the house on his father's farm in 1920, the year that he and Bernice McMurry married. It was an unpainted frame structure, with two large rooms: a kitchen, and a bedroom, which was heated by an open fireplace. There was also a large front porch, where everyone gathered in the evening, except during the colder days of winter. It was small by white standards, but extremely large by black ones at the time, and the Scotts even had a well in the backyard, which furnished them water all year round. Almost everyone else in the all-black community, just outside the small town of Heiberger, had to carry water from a nearby creek back to where they lived.

Just then, the front door opened, and Obie Scott stuck his head inside. "How's Mrs. Scott doing?" he asked.

"She's doing just fine, Brother Scott," Mrs. Holden said.

Suddenly, there was a loud wail from the bedroom, and Mr. Scott's eyes began to glow.

"Congratulations, Brother Scott," Mrs. Franklin said. "You're a new father."

The three churchwomen stood up, walked to the bedroom door, and went inside.

The baby was a girl. The Scotts named her Coretta, after Mr. Scott's mother, Cora. In her home, and among her extended family and friends, Coretta would be loved and cared for as though she were one of the most important people in the world. It would only be later, outside this safe environment, when she would come to realize that the color of her skin kept her from enjoying all the rights and privileges that white people had.

On October 29, 1929, when Coretta was two and a half years old, an event in New York City began what was, for the United States, the Great Depression. With the "crash" of the stock market, the American economy almost collapsed. Banks and businesses closed all over the country. People lost their homes and their jobs and went hungry.

"What's going to happen to us, Obie?" Mrs. Scott asked her husband one evening at the supper table.

Edythe and Coretta looked expectantly at their father. Edythe, now almost five, had been telling Coretta all day what she had been hearing on the radio, and Coretta was scared. According to Edythe, they might have to move and live somewhere in a tent. Coretta had started crying when she heard that. She didn't want to leave her home.

"It's hard to tell," Mr. Scott said, putting his fork down. "Some of the people in Heiberger are talking about going to Birmingham, while others are talking about going down to Mobile."

"I don't want to go anywhere, Daddy," Coretta said.

Mr. Scott smiled. "We're not leaving, Coretta, so don't you start worrying," he said.

"We're more fortunate than most people are."

"How can that be, Daddy?" Edythe asked. "I keep hearing people say that whites are better than us."

Mrs. Scott pursed her lips. "That's not what they're talking about, Edythe," she said. "They're talking about the color of your skin."

"What does that matter?" Edythe asked.

"It doesn't matter at all, except to some white people," Mr. Scott said, "but there are also some very kind white people who don't feel that way, so never forget that."

"I never want either of you to judge a person by the color of his skin," Mrs. Scott said. "It's what people do with their lives that matters and how people treat one another. That's what makes a person good or bad."

"The Good Lord has blessed us with our own home, some animals to help feed us, and some water to quench our thirsts," Mr. Scott said. "You girls always remember that."

Mrs. Scott stood up and grinned at the girls. "We've also been blessed with strong bodies, which allow us to work hard," she said, "and now, we need to use those strong bodies to clear the table and wash the dishes."

Coretta always liked helping her mother in the kitchen. She sometimes stood on a wooden stool beside the counter where her mother put the dishpans, one with soapy water for washing, one with clean water for rinsing, and listened to the stories about each plate. Many of them, Coretta learned, were given to her parents when they married. Almost none of them were new, because few family members could afford it, but the fact that they had been used meant they always had an interesting history.

"This platter belonged to your grandfather Jeff Scott's grandmother," Mrs. Scott said. "She told him that, during the Civil War, some Yankee soldiers stole it from a white woman whose house she cleaned, and then

they threw it in a ditch a mile or so down the road."

"What's a 'Yankee,' Mama?" Edythe asked.

"That's what white folks in the South called Union soldiers, the ones from up north," Mrs. Scott said. "Your great-great-grandmother found the platter, unbroken, then took it back to the woman's house. But the woman said she didn't want anything that some Yankee had touched, so she give it to your great-great-grandmother, and that's how your grandfather came to have it."

"I'm glad the Yankees threw it away," Coretta said. She gently put the platter into the rinse water, swirled it around, then handed it to Edythe to dry. "It's so pretty."

By the time the dishes were finished, Coretta had heard family stories about all of them.

In 1930, three-year-old Coretta became a big sister when Obadiah Leonard was born. Right away, Coretta, who was getting a reputation in the family for being "bossy," started telling "Obie Leonard" what he should do and what he shouldn't do. Often, she told him to stop crying, especially when her mother sang them lullabies. Even though the lullaby was meant to put Obie Leonard to sleep, Coretta had decided that the song was just as much for her as it was for her brother.

Mrs. Scott had only received a fourth-grade education, but she loved music and so had taught herself how to sing. She had a beautiful voice. At church, other members often spoke about Mrs. Scott's voice. They said that she sounded like an angel and that she was more talented than many of the singers on records or the radio. Mrs. Scott just smiled and never let any of the praise go to her head. She was also beginning to see in Coretta the same appreciation for music she had, so instead of scolding Coretta when she tried to shush Obie Leonard, Mrs. Scott would make sure that she would make time to sit with Coretta and sing to her.

• • •

As the Depression continued to grip the country, the hardworking Scotts not only survived but actually lived better than some of the poorer whites in the county. Mr. Scott was one of the few black men who owned his own truck and, during the day, he used it to haul logs for some of the white sawmill owners in the area that helped him earn extra money.

By the time Coretta was six, in 1933, she was working alongside her mother, her sister, and even her brother in the gardens and the fields on their farm. Although it was hard, Coretta never complained. She knew what she was doing meant not only that her family had food but that other families in the community did too, because the Scotts were generous.

"I need to sharpen my hoe, Mama," Coretta said. "It's too dull to cut any of these weeds."

Mrs. Scott put down her own hoe, took a file out of the canvas pouch she had slung over one shoulder, and began sharpening Coretta's hoe blade.

Coretta watched as the dark brown edge turned a bright silver, looking much like the knives in their kitchen.

"This should be better," Mrs. Scott said. She handed the hoe back to Coretta. "No weed will be safe from you now."

Coretta laughed and struck a large weed in the row just ahead of her. She sliced it off almost to the roots. "Now, it won't take any of the food out of the ground that the corn needs," she said, something she had learned from her father when she had asked him why she needed to hoe in the first place.

For the rest of the afternoon the family took care of the garden. Coretta made the time go faster for everyone by singing hymns from church and songs she made up.

By the end of the summer, Coretta and Edythe were taking care of the gardens and the crops by themselves. On the weekends, when Mr. Scott wasn't hauling lumber, he joined them, and that was when Coretta enjoyed it the most. She never heard her parents complain about anything. Instead, Coretta was constantly reminded that the Good Lord had smiled on them and that it was their responsibility to take care of what they had been given to the best of their abilities.

One night, when Mr. Scott usually got home from work, Coretta went with him to feed the cows, as she often did. She had even been allowed to name each one.

"Bessie looks sad," Coretta said one evening. "What's wrong with her?"

"It could be something she ate, Coretta," Mr. Scott said. "There are some weeds in the field that aren't good for her. The rest of the cows mostly stay away from them, but maybe Bessie wasn't paying attention."

Coretta knew that could be the case. Of

all the cows, Bessie was the one who seemed to be the dreamer. Coretta thought that was why she liked her so much. Coretta liked to dream too, about all the things she wanted to do when she grew up.

Just as Coretta and her father reached the chicken pen, on their way back to the house, Edythe was coming out of it with a basket of eggs. "There aren't as many tonight as there should be, Daddy," she said. "I think that silly snake has been at it again."

"Maybe, maybe not," Mr. Scott said. "Sometimes hens just don't feel like laying."

Coretta didn't like gathering the eggs. Once, when she had stuck her hand into one of the higher nests, she had touched a snake, and had run screaming back to the house. It didn't matter that her mother said that it was only a gray rat snake and that it was more interested in the eggs than it was in Coretta. She never wanted to see that snake again.

Remembering the experience, though, made Coretta shiver, and she took hold of her father's hand as they let the aroma of ham hock and red beans lead them to the kitchen door.

No More Lies—If I Can Help It

"I'll eat your potatoes if you don't want them," seven-year-old Coretta said to Edythe one Sunday dinner.

"You don't need any more starch, Coretta," Mrs. Scott told her. "You could barely fasten that dress for Sunday school this morning."

Coretta took a deep breath and sucked in her stomach. "It feels just fine now, Mama," she said, "so may I have Edythe's potatoes if she's not going to eat them?"

Mr. Scott shook his head. "Let her have them, Edythe, if you're truly not going to eat them all, because we are not going to waste any food," he said. "If Coretta plans to hold her breath from now on so her dress will fit, then I guess we shouldn't worry about it."

Coretta let out her breath with a loud noise, then said, "Oh, all right, I don't have to have them if everybody is going to make fun of me!" She noisily scooted her chair back so she could get up from the table, but Mr. Scott calmly said, "I don't remember your asking permission to be excused, Coretta."

Coretta flared her nostrils, but she knew better than to talk back to her parents, so she said, "May I please be excused?"

"You may," Mr. Scott said, "and you may also go outside to wait for your cousins."

This time, Coretta pushed the chair out quietly, then slid it back under the table, as her mother had taught her, and headed out to the front porch. Besides church services, the only thing Coretta enjoyed more on Sundays than dinner were the visits from her many relatives. She sat in the wooden seat swing, using her patent leather shoes to push it back and forth, trying not to scuff them. They were hand-me-downs from a cousin who lived in Birmingham, and Coretta knew that if she ruined them, she'd never get another pair. These were so shiny, she could see her face in them. She quickly took one off, held it up like a mirror, and then, with a disgusted sigh, dropped it onto the porch.

So what if I am fat? she thought. *I can still outrun or outclimb everybody I know.*

Just then, Coretta spotted a cloud of dust far down the road that went past their house. She was sure that meant a wagon and a team of horses belonging to one of her uncles was headed their way. Coretta had so many relatives, that she never paid any attention to whose side of the family her cousins belonged to.

Coretta stood up and opened the front door. "I see them coming!" she shouted.

Edythe and Obie Leonard came out onto the porch to wait with her.

"Wait!" Coretta said. "I'm going to change clothes. I can't have any fun in this dress."

"You'd better not do that, Coretta," Edythe warned her. "Mama likes for you to look nice when we have company."

"I can look nice in my work clothes," Coretta told her.

Coretta didn't wait to hear what Edythe said in response. Instead, she hurried inside, went into the bedroom, and pulled her work clothes out of a box she kept under the bed. By the time she had changed and was back out on the front porch, her parents were greeting her aunt and uncle and their five children.

Coretta was a little disappointed—they weren't her favorite cousins. But they were the ones who had come for a Sunday visit, and they were better than nothing.

"Hi, Mary!" Coretta called. "Hi, Zachariah!" Mary and Zachariah were the closest to her in age, although Mary was a few months older, and she made sure Coretta didn't forget it.

Coretta ran to the big mocker-nut hickory tree and climbed up to her special branch. "What do you want to do?" she shouted down to them.

Mary wasn't paying any attention to her, but Zachariah shrugged his shoulders. After a few minutes, Coretta climbed back down and went over to where they were standing. "Do you want to go out to the fields and have a race?" she asked.

"I guess," Zachariah said. He turned to his sister. "Come on, Mary."

"Do I look like I'm ready for a race?" Mary said. She brushed her dress. "I don't want to get dirty."

"I'll race you!"

Coretta turned to see a girl she hadn't noticed before. "Who are you?" she asked.

"This is my friend Suz," Mary said. "We took her to church with us this morning, and she wanted to come with us to see you."

"Suz says she can beat you at running and at climbing trees, Coretta," Zachariah said.

"Well, then come on," Coretta said to Suz. "We'll just see if you can."

Coretta started running toward the cornfield. Suz was right behind her. When the two of them reached the first stand of stalks, Coretta said, "You're pretty good, but I still think I can beat you."

"It's a bet," Suz said. "What are you going to give me when I win?"

"I'm not going to give you anything, because you're not going to win," Coretta said. She looked back toward Zachariah, who had slowed down and was huffing and puffing. "Hurry up!" she yelled at him. "We can't wait all day."

When Zachariah finally reached them, Coretta said, "We'll line up right here, then we'll race between these rows of corn to the fence, all right?"

"All right," Suz said.

Zachariah seemed to have trouble catching his breath.

"Maybe you'd better just stay here," Coretta said.

Zachariah nodded. "I'll be the referee and tell you when to go," he said.

Coretta and Suz lined up.

"On your mark, get ready, get set, GO!" Zachariah shouted.

Coretta and Suz took off. At first, Coretta thought she'd have the advantage, because she was used to running the rows of corn, but Suz was able to keep up with her. For the next

few minutes they ran neck and neck. Then Suz bumped Coretta and threw her off balance.

"Hey!" Coretta shouted. She tried to regain her balance, but her left foot caught on the bottom of a stalk and she stumbled. "Stop! You did that on purpose!"

"No, I didn't," Suz shouted back. She continued running. "You're just clumsy."

Coretta was furious. This had never happened to her before. Instead of trying to catch up with Suz, though, she hunted around in the adjoining rows of corn until she had found several rocks and sticks. Then she crawled back over to the row where they had been racing and waited for Suz to return.

After a few minutes, Coretta heard Suz coming back. Just as Suz came even with where Coretta was hidden, Coretta started throwing the rocks and sticks at her.

"Ouch! Ouch! Ouch!" Suz cried. She stopped and looked around, trying to figure out what had happened.

All of a sudden, Coretta dashed out from her hiding place and began racing back down the row toward Zachariah. Behind her, Coretta could hear Suz calling her bad names.

When Coretta finally spotted Zachariah, she shouted, "I won! I won!"

"So what?" Zachariah said. "You always win."

Just then, Suz ran up, screaming at Coretta, "You cheated. You're a terrible person! You threw rocks and sticks at me!"

"Well, you pushed me!" Coretta shouted back.

"No, I didn't!" Suz said. Now, tears were streaming down her face. "You're just clumsy, and you're a bad sport, too!"

"I'm going to tell on you, Coretta," Zachariah said.

"I don't care," Coretta said. "I don't like to play with you, anyway!"

Coretta watched as Zachariah and Suz ran

back to her house. She knew what was in store for her now, but she didn't want to think about it. She didn't know why she couldn't control her temper. It was always getting her in trouble.

When Coretta got back to the house, her mother was waiting for her on the back porch. She looked at Coretta and sighed. Then she turned around and went inside. Coretta followed.

"Sit down, Coretta," Mrs. Scott said gently. Coretta sat. "You simply have to learn how to behave like a young lady," Mrs. Scott continued, "and young ladies do not throw sticks and stones at other young ladies."

"Suz is no young lady, Mama," Coretta said. "She pushed me on purpose, and that's the truth."

"Well, there are better ways to handle arguments than doing what you did," Mrs. Scott said. "I want you to sit here and think about what some of them might be."

"Yes, Mama," Coretta said. "I'm sorry, and I'll think about those ways, I truly will."

That evening, after the relatives were gone, the Scott family ate a meal of leftovers from Sunday dinner, and then they all went back out on the front porch. During spring and summer evenings, especially, this was one of the family times that Coretta enjoyed most.

Under the tree, Mrs. Scott read to them from one of their favorite books. "Tonight, it's going to be the story of Rumpelstiltskin," she announced.

Coretta was in her usual place on the wooden seat swing, snuggled up against her father. With the night sounds of insects all around them, she was ready for her mother's voice to whisk her off to a magical place.

"There was once a miller who was poor, but who had a beautiful daughter," Mrs. Scott began, and for the next several minutes they all listened as the miller told the king that his daughter could spin straw into gold, and how a tiny character named Rumplestiltskin actually spun it, but for a heavy price.

When Mrs. Scott finished, she asked, "What do you think the moral of that story is?"

"If you lie, you'll be punished," Edythe said.

"I think that's a good answer," Mr. Scott said.

Coretta snuggled closer to her father, wondering if the story had been specially chosen for her. She promised herself that she'd never lie again, if she could help it.

Mrs. Scott closed the book and said, "Well, I'd like to hear some music. What about the rest of you?"

"Me too!" Coretta shouted. Nothing soothed her soul like a good song. When music was playing, all of the things that made her angry seemed to disappear.

"Let me choose it, Mama," Coretta said.

"We wouldn't think of letting anyone else," Edythe said, grinning.

Everyone in the family knew how important music was to Coretta.

The Scotts owned a windup Victrola record player, something no other black family in the community had, and something even white families prized highly. The Scotts loved all kinds of music: hymns, popular songs, and jazz. Over the years they had spent some of their hard-earned money on long-playing record albums of such famous band leaders as Glen Gray, the Dorsey Brothers, and Guy Lombardo, and such famous singers as Bing Crosby and Ethel Merman. Coretta always took the greatest care with the records. She gently removed them from their sleeves, then wiped them with a special cloth before putting them on the turntable. After she had wound up the Victrola she carefully put the needle arm in the first groove, and returned to the porch.

As Glen Gray and the Casa Loma Orchestra began playing "Avalon," Coretta started to sing. For the next several minutes the entire Scott family was transported from the front porch of their house in rural Alabama to the bright lights of New York City. Coretta followed "Avalon" with "In the Still of the Night" and "One of Us Was Wrong."

After Coretta stopped singing, no one said anything for a few minutes, and the only sounds came from the insects, then Mrs. Scott said, "You're just a different person when you're singing, honey, and I mean everything good by that. You just. . . well, you just have the ability to take us all to a different place."

Mr. Scott, Edythe, and even Obie Leonard murmured their agreement.

"Thank you," Coretta said. "I love to sing."

Coretta put on another record, and they all hummed along with the tunes. When it was over, Mr. Scott said, "Well, the moon has gone behind the clouds, turning out the light, so I guess that means it's telling us it's time to go to bed."

That night, in her bed, Coretta didn't dream about the arguments she'd had that day. Instead, she dreamed about becoming a famous singer.

It Isn't Fair

"Hurry up, Coretta, we haven't got all day," Mr. Scott said. "We need to drive into Marion, take care of our business, and then get back. You can't leave a farm very long. The animals don't understand it."

Eight-year-old Coretta giggled. "I'm hurry-ing, Daddy," she said.

The trips into Marion, about twelve miles away from their farm, were always a special treat. Edythe had told her that Marion wasn't nearly as large as Birmingham, at least from the pictures she'd seen, but Coretta thought Marion had everything she could ever want.

When everyone was ready, Mr. and Mrs. Scott got into the cab of the truck, with Obie Leonard sitting between them, and Edythe and Coretta climbed into the back and sat on a wooden bench built especially for such trips, flush against the rear window. Coretta loved watching the countryside fly by as they headed toward town. It reminded her of carnival rides she'd seen pictures of. She knew that once in a while carnivals came to Marion, but one time, when she had asked her father to take them so they could go on the Ferris wheel, he told her they didn't have the money to waste. Later, Edythe told her it was really because black people weren't allowed to go on the rides.

The road into Marion, Lafayette Street, took them by some of the larger houses in the town, and Coretta always wondered what they looked like inside. She had heard before that only white people lived in them, but once, when she had seen a black woman coming out of one of the houses, she asked her mother if black people lived in some of them too.

"No, Coretta, no black people live around here, only white people," Mrs. Scott told her. "If you saw a black woman coming out of one of those houses, honey, then that just means she works there."

Coretta knew that black people cleaned for white people, took care of their children, cooked their meals, washed their clothes and, in general, did whatever white people needed them to do.

"Why do they want us around so much if they don't think we're as good as they are?" Coretta asked.

Edythe looked over at her. "What are you talking about?" she said.

"Nothing," Coretta said. She had suddenly decided that she didn't want to ruin her trip to Marion by thinking about bad things like that.

34

At the intersection of Lafayette and Washington streets, Mr. Scott turned right, drove two blocks, and parked his truck in front of Edwards' Mercantile Store.

"I'm going to take Obie Leonard with me," Mr. Scott said. "You women can do your shopping here, and I'll be back for you in an hour."

Coretta really wanted to go with her father. She knew he visited with some of the white men in the town, always trying to find extra jobs to support his family. With the country still in the Depression, it was difficult, but Coretta also knew that her father was one of the hardest working men in the county and that the white men knew this.

As Coretta, Edythe, and Mrs. Scott approached the front door to Edwards' Mercantile Store a white woman and her daughter walked in front of them, gave them hostile stares, and went inside, almost letting the door hit Mrs. Scott in the face.

"What are they doing here?" Coretta heard

the girl ask her mother. "I thought colored people weren't allowed in white stores."

Coretta bit down on her lower lip to keep from saying anything to the girl, but it was difficult not to. She knew that if she'd said something, though, nothing would have changed the girl's attitude toward them.

Once inside, Coretta made herself forget the incident. She looked around—she was positive that she could find anything in this store that she would ever need. Now, all she wanted was to be left alone so she could wander around.

Edythe always went with Mrs. Scott to look at the bolts of cloth, but Coretta walked up and down the different aisles slowly, thinking what it would be like to have enough money to buy anything in here that she liked. She almost always ended up at the back of the store, where there were long-playing records and sheet music for the piano. Coretta knew Mrs. Edwards didn't really mind her taking the sheet music out of the racks so she could look inside at the notes. Although Coretta couldn't read them, she was fascinated by their shapes, and she knew that one of these days, she would know what sounds they made. Coretta also liked to look at the pictures of famous singers or band leaders on the front of the sheet music or the covers of the record albums. If she tried hard enough, Coretta was able to change the face of whatever woman she was looking at to her face. Then she became that person dressed in a beautiful evening gown, standing on a small stage, in front of a microphone, and singing the latest popular song.

All of a sudden a white arm appeared in front of her and brought her back to the present. The arm belonged to the rude girl who had pushed in front of them when they had first entered the store.

"You need to move," the girl said to her. "I can't reach the sheet music."

"Well, I'm looking at it too," Coretta said, "so you'll just have to wait your turn."

The girl gasped, opened her mouth to say something, then closed it and walked away. Coretta saw her head straight for her mother, where she angrily told her, Coretta was sure, what had just happened. Right away, the woman went to Mrs. Edwards, who was standing at a counter, and shouted something to her. Coretta saw Mrs. Edwards look at her, shake her head, then say something to the woman, which seemed to calm her down, but the woman and the girl left, anyway.

Just then, Edythe came over and said, "Mama wants to show you some cloth, to see what you want for your dress."

"That white girl told me to move away from the sheet music so she could look at it," Coretta said as she and Edythe headed toward the notions area. "I told her I was looking too."

"You need to keep your mouth shut,"

Edythe said. "It's going to get the family in trouble one of these days."

Coretta knew that Edythe was right, but she didn't see why she should have to stop what she was doing just because the white girl had told her to. After all, she was there first.

Mrs. Scott had pulled several bolts of cloth from the shelf and had them ready to show Coretta, but Coretta was no longer in the mood to look at them. Instead, she said, "Why do you have to make our dresses, Mama?" She pointed to a row of ready-made ones hanging on a rack in the next aisle. "Why can't we just buy some of those instead?"

"Well, for one thing, Coretta, they cost more money," Mrs. Scott said. "And for another, you'd have to try it on, to make sure it fit, and we colored folks aren't allowed to do that."

"Well, I'm going . . . ," Coretta started to say, but just then Mrs. Edwards walked up and said, "Have you decided yet, Bernice?"

40

"No, ma'am, Mrs. Edwards," Mrs. Scott said. "We're still thinking about it."

"Well, hurry up, because if you handle this cloth too much and some of my white customers see it, I'll have to put it all on the sale table," Mrs. Edwards said.

"We took baths last night," Coretta said. "We're not dirty."

Mrs. Edwards blinked in surprise. "Well, I'm sure you did, Coretta, I'm sure you did, but . . ." She let out a big sigh and turned to Mrs. Scott. "Bernice, Coretta made Mrs. DeKalb very angry just a few minutes ago," she said. "The DeKalbs spend a lot of money in here, and I just don't want Coretta talking back to their daughter. If she doesn't—"

"I'll take five yards of this blue pattern," Mrs. Scott said hurriedly, "and six yards of this yellow pattern."

Without saying anything else, Mrs. Edwards picked up the two bolts, carried them to the front counter, cut off the material, put it in a paper bag, handed it to Mrs. Scott, and said, "That'll be two dollars."

Mrs. Scott paid for the material, then she left the store with Edythe and Coretta.

Mr. Scott was just pulling up in front of the store.

"She overcharged you for the material, Mama," Edythe said.

"No, she didn't, Edythe," Mrs. Scott said. "Colored people have to pay more than white people."

Mrs. Scott got into the cab, and Edythe and Coretta climbed into the back again and sat on the bench.

As they headed back down Washington Street, Coretta said, "Why did Mrs. Edwards call Mama 'Bernice' and Mrs. DeKalb 'Mrs. DeKalb'?"

"Why do you think, Coretta?" Edythe said.

The stores that had created so much excitement for Coretta before seemed so uninviting all of a sudden. She no longer wanted to look at them, and she could hardly wait until they got back home, but after a few minutes, Mr. Scott stopped the truck in front of DeKalb's Farm Supply Store and got out.

"Come on, Coretta," Mr. Scott said. "I'll need some help carrying things back to the truck."

"Can't you buy what you need somewhere else, Daddy?" Coretta said. She knew the store belonged to the father of the rude girl who had been in the mercantile store. "Why do you have to spend your money here?"

Mr. Scott gave her a funny look. "Well, it's the only store in Marion that sells what I need," he said.

Reluctantly, Coretta jumped off the truck bed and followed her father inside.

"What did you need, boy?" a white man at the back of the store called. He was sitting on a wooden barrel and looking straight at Coretta's father.

Coretta noticed that her father didn't

answer right away but instead walked straight to the back of the store, keeping his eyes on the man as he did so. The man didn't move, but Coretta saw that he had begun to look a little nervous.

When Coretta's father reached the man, he stood in front of him and said, "I'm Mr. Scott, and I need a salt lick for my cows, a new plow blade for my plow, and two sacks of chicken feed."

The man blinked once, looked as though he wanted to say something but didn't, and then hopped down off the barrel and got the items Coretta's father had requested.

After Mr. Scott had paid for them, he said, "I'd appreciate it very much if you'd help me carry these things out to my truck."

Again, Coretta knew that the man wanted to decline, but he didn't, and with Mr. Scott carrying the two bags of chicken feed, the man carrying the plow blade, and Coretta the salt lick, they headed outside.

44

After the farm supplies were stacked on the bed of the truck, the man stepped back and said, "Whose truck is this, boy?"

Mr. Scott looked at the man and said, "It's mine."

The man opened his mouth to say something else, but Mr. Scott said, "Now, for a treat, girls." He got into the cab, started the engine, and drove off.

Coretta watched the white man, still staring at them, his mouth open, get smaller and smaller, until they turned a corner.

When Coretta told Edythe what had happened, Edythe said, "Daddy always says that if you look a white man in the eyes, he can't hurt you."

"Well, it worked this time," Coretta said, "but I'm not sure it'll work every time."

In a few minutes, Mr. Scott parked in front of Perry's Drug Store, and they all got out of the truck. As they headed around the corner, to a side door, Coretta saw several white boys and girls her age going in the front entrance. It didn't make sense to her that, because of the color of her skin, she couldn't do that. Still, what she really wanted now was an ice-cream cone, and she decided not to think about where she had to go to get it.

The Scott family entered a side door that said COLOREDS ONLY and stood at the small counter. Mr. Perry was working today, dressed in his white cap and white apron, joking with the customers as he dipped ice-cream cones for them. Coretta wished it had been Mrs. Perry or even their son, Franklin, because they were always a little nicer to her. It seemed like it took forever for Mr. Perry to come over and take their orders, because he waited on several white people who had come in after the Scotts. Finally, he sauntered over to them and said, "What do you want?"

Mr. and Mrs. Scott ordered vanilla, Obie Leonard and Edythe ordered strawberry, and Coretta ordered chocolate. Mr. Perry told Mr.

Scott he had to pay first, which he did.

When Mr. Perry returned with the five cones, Coretta noticed the dips were all orange looking.

The Scotts all took their cones and left the building—except for Coretta.

"This isn't chocolate," she said. "I ordered chocolate!"

"If you don't want it, girl, then you can toss it in that trash can over there," Mr. Perry said, "but you're not getting your money back."

Coretta felt like throwing the ice cream in Mr. Perry's face, but it was still ice cream, so she decided it was better than nothing. As Coretta left the building, she took a couple of licks and frowned. It tasted terrible.

When Coretta got back to the truck, she said, "Why didn't Mr. Perry give us what we ordered?"

"If white people don't like a particular flavor that Mr. Perry has ordered for his store, Coretta, he gives it to us no matter what we order, rather than lose money on it," Mrs. Scott said. "Sometimes we're lucky and they like all his flavors, but today we weren't."

As they headed home, Coretta decided to make a list of all the things that white people could do but that she and her family couldn't. Before they had even left the city limits of Marion, though, the list had grown so long that she couldn't remember everything.

I'm Going to Make People Change

Whenever Coretta complained to her mother about how white people treated them, her mother always said, "You're just as good as anyone else in Perry County, Coretta, and if you get a good education, then white people can't kick you around anymore and you won't have to depend on them for jobs, either."

"I want to be even better, Mama," Coretta

said. "I want to be good as the rest of the people in the United States."

No matter what, Mrs. Scott would always end their conversations with, "Study harder, then."

Coretta liked school, up to a point—except when the buses carrying the white children stirred up the dust and covered their clean clothes with it, then that was all she could think about for the rest of the day, that and how she couldn't even drink from the water fountain outside the Perry County Courthouse in Marion, when she was really thirsty on hot days.

That evening, Coretta knew she should be doing her math homework, but when her father started toward the front door, she said, "Where are you going, Daddy?"

"Just over to Mr. Thomas's mercantile store, Coretta, because I don't have time to go into Marion," Mr. Scott said. "The harness broke on the plow horse, so I need to get a new one, but I don't want to drive into Marion, and I need to pick up a few grocery items too."

"Will you take me along?" Coretta asked.

"Have you finished your assignment, Coretta?" Mrs. Scott asked.

"Almost, Mama," Coretta said. "I can work the rest of the problems out in my head on the way."

Mrs. Scott sighed. "Well, all right, just make sure you do," she said.

"I'll help you, Coretta," Mr. Scott said.

By the time they were halfway to Mr. Thomas's store, Coretta had almost finished what she had said she'd do, so she decided she could afford to devote some of her attention just to being with her father. He was such a good man, and he worked so hard for them, but he sometimes seemed sad, especially when he didn't think anyone was looking at him.

"Why do like Mr. Thomas so much?" Coretta

asked. "What has he ever done for us?"

"Coretta Scott! I won't have you take that attitude about Mr. Thomas," Mr. Scott said. "He's a good man, and if it hadn't been for him, well, I might have lost my truck when the Depression started."

Mr. Scott explained to Coretta that Mr. Thomas now held the mortgage on the truck and that Mr. Thomas didn't pay Mr. Scott for his work at the lumber mill but instead paid the bank each month what Mr. Scott would have owed them. He also said that Mr. Thomas let them buy things from his store on credit if they didn't have enough money during the month, and that that, too, was counted as part of what he earned at the lumberyard.

Although Coretta didn't say anything, she knew that her father also hauled lumber for Mr. Thomas, and while Mr. Thomas did pay him for that, he never paid him enough, and her father was always having to look for other ways to earn money for the family. To do this, he needed to work on nights and weekends.

No matter how nice her father thought Mr. Thomas was, Coretta knew that Mr. Thomas had made it so that her father could probably never be completely debt free.

Mr. Scott pulled into a parking space in front of the mercantile store and said, "I'm glad you came with me, Coretta. I enjoy your company."

"Thank you, Daddy," Coretta said. "I'm glad I came too."

Together, they entered the mercantile store, and right away Coretta heard, "Good evening, Obie!" It was one of the friendliest greetings Coretta had ever heard from a white person, but then she knew that since her father owed the man so much money, that Mr. Thomas certainly didn't want to anger him. Of course, Coretta guessed if her father ever did anger Mr. Thomas, the law would be on Mr. Thomas's side.

Just as Coretta and Mr. Scott reached the

back of the store, Mr. Thomas said good-bye to another customer, a man who didn't even look at them. Almost at the same time, though, a woman pushed aside a curtain and came through a door behind where the sales counter was.

"Well, good evening to you, Mr. Scott," the woman said. She looked at Coretta. "And who is this?"

"This is Coretta, our middle child, Mrs. Thomas," Mr. Scott said. He looked at Coretta and nodded, letting her know that she shouldn't just stand there, that she should return the greeting, so Coretta said, "Good evening to you, Mrs. Thomas."

It wasn't that she didn't have manners, Coretta wanted to tell the Thomases, it was just that she was so bowled over by how nice they were, she was almost speechless.

Later, after they had the harness and the groceries and were headed back to the house, Coretta said, "I still think he's almost like a plantation owner, Daddy, and even if he's nice to us, we're still his slaves."

"That's enough, Coretta," Mr. Scott said. "I've told you before that if you look a white man in the eye, he can't hurt you, and I always look Mr. Thomas in the eye."

So Coretta dropped the subject and started thinking about finishing the rest of her math problems.

A week later, though, when Coretta went into Marion with two of her aunts, Bessie and Loretta, she once again was shown the ugly side of life in the South.

The three of them were going to see another one of Coretta's aunts—Thelma, Bessie and Loretta's sister, who had recently moved to Marion. Thelma had a job cleaning house for Mr. and Mrs. H. G. Thigpen, who owned H. G. Thigpen's Groceries and Hardware. Taking Loretta's team of horses and a hay wagon, they headed into Marion. When they got to the Thigpens' house, Thelma was sitting out on the front porch. She ran out to the wagon and jumped onto it.

"Aren't you going to show us where your room is?" Bessie asked.

"I can't," Thelma said. "Mr. and Mrs. Thigpen won't allow me to have company."

Loretta raised an eyebrow. "So where do you and your man, Rolly, go to talk?" she asked.

"We usually walk in the park," Thelma said. "There's a colored section where the white people don't bother you."

"That is so silly!" Coretta said.

Her three aunts just looked at her. Then Bessie said, "Coretta's getting kind of uppity, don't you think?"

"I sure do," Thelma said. They all three laughed.

But Coretta didn't see anything funny about it at all, and she didn't think her aunts should either.

"I need to go to Thigpen's," Thelma said.

"We're at the Thigpens', girl," Bessie said. "Did you think we'd been driving around while you were talking?"

That set the three of them laughing again. Even Coretta had to smile.

"No, no, I mean their grocery and hardware store," Thelma said.

Loretta picked up the reins and said, "Just tell me how to get there and I'll relay the message to George and Shelby."

"George and Shelby!" Thelma said. "You named these horses after your boyfriends!"

"We sure did," Bessie said. "This is the only way we could ever get them to do what we tell them to do."

Now, Coretta joined her aunts in laughing so hard, they all four had to bend over to catch their breath.

With Thelma's direction, they soon reached Thigpen's, and Loretta tied up the horses to a hitching post on the sidewalk.

As they headed toward the front door, Coretta pulled back. "We'd better go in the back way, hadn't we," she said, "or we'll cause some trouble."

"We're not causing any trouble," Thelma said. "If I'm shopping for Mrs. Thigpen, I always go in the front way."

Coretta reluctantly followed, making sure she stayed behind them, just in case. She couldn't figure out why white people were so unpredictable when it came to how they treated them.

As they entered the store, Coretta held her breath, but when nothing happened right away, she stepped out from behind her aunts so she could see what was going on. Thigpen's didn't look as large of some of the other stores she'd seen in Marion, but it was neat and clean.

"What are you doing here, Thelma?" a voice called from the back of the store.

"Mrs. Thigpen needs some Omega Flour,

sir," Thelma said. "She was supposed to telephone you."

"Well, she didn't, but go ahead and get one of those ten-pound bags off that bottom shelf on the far wall," Mr. Thipgen said. "You might as well pick up a can of baking soda, too, and maybe some salt. I think we're low on those things."

"Yes, sir, Mr. Thigpen," Thelma said.

Coretta followed her three aunts to the far side of the store. Something Bessie said to Loretta made her laugh, then Loretta pointed to a shelf, and Bessie laughed too.

Just then, an elderly white woman stepped in front of them and said, "You girls need to be quieter. I can hardly hear myself think, you're making so much noise. Why don't you stop your silly chattering, so you can get out of here."

"They were just having some fun," Coretta said. "Are you afraid it'll crack your face if you try to laugh?"

The white woman's intake of breath was

loud enough to be heard all over the store. "Why, I have never in all my life heard such impertinence," she managed to say. "How dare you . . ."

Just then, Mr. Thigpen appeared and said, "What's wrong, Mrs. Knox?"

"She called my aunts 'girls,'" Coretta said in a strong voice. "They're not 'girls,' they're *ladies*, and they're just as important as . . . as *Mrs. Knox* here!"

Mrs. Knox's face was now a bright red.

"I'm sorry, Mrs. Knox," Mr. Thigpen said. He turned and shouted, "Sally! Come here! Mrs. Knox needs your help to finish her shopping!" When he looked back at Coretta and her aunts, his lips were pursed tightly. He took a deep breath, exhaled slowly, and then said, "Thelma, I want you to get the things that Mrs. Thigpen sent you after, and then I want you to leave this store, and I never, ever, want you to come in here again accompanied by anyone. Do you understand me?"

"Yes, sir, Mr. Thigpen," Thelma said, "I most certainly do."

Thelma quickly got the items, then, without even waiting for Mr. Thigpen to put them in a bag, left the store with Coretta and her aunts.

No one said a word until they were out of sight of Mr. Thigpen's store, then Thelma said, "Well, I'll probably be looking for another job tomorrow."

"I'm sorry, Aunt Thelma," Coretta said. "I shouldn't have opened my mouth."

Thelma smiled at her. "You only did what I've been wanting to do for a long time, Coretta," she said. "Nobody has the right to talk to us that way, nobody, and I think your aunts should be more like you."

That evening, back at home, Coretta told her parents what had happened in Marion.

For a few minutes, neither one said anything, then Mrs. Scott said, "Well, Coretta, you're either going to have a very difficult life, or you're going to be the reason for some big changes in the way white folks treat us."

"Mama, I'm going to have a good life, that I truly believe," Coretta said, "so I guess I'd better start thinking about how I'm going to make people change."

After supper, Mr. Scott said, "I want to show everyone something." He opened a paper bag and took out a pair of scissors, a trimmer, and some pomade, and added, "I'm going to teach myself how to give haircuts so I can make some extra money."

"Daddy!" Coretta said. "When are you going to have time to do that? You work all day at the lumbermill, then you haul lumber at night, and on the weekends you work in the fields here. You never rest."

"It's true, Daddy," Edythe said. "Why are you doing this?"

"Well, I have a dream," Mr. Scott said. "I

want us to have a bigger house, and if I save the money I can make off cutting hair, then that dream might just come true."

At that moment, Coretta realized that she had just learned another lesson from her parents: If you want something bad enough, then you work hard and you save your money, and your dreams will come true.

"Well, Daddy, I think it's a wonderful idea," Coretta said, "and since my hair is a little longer than I like it, I'll let you practice on me!"

Out of Debt

Just one more row, nine-year-old Coretta thought, *and I'll not only be finished picking cotton for the day but I'll get paid, too.* A few feet away from her was an older black woman whom everyone called Aunt Lily. Coretta couldn't understand how anyone that frail could drag a long ticking sack through the fields, especially when it was so full of cotton that it was ready to burst at the seams.

Once, Coretta had even offered to help Aunt Lily as they neared the end of the row where the cotton was dumped out into a trailer before it was taken to be ginned, but Aunt Lily had scolded her and reminded her that she'd been doing this long before Coretta was born, and she didn't need any of her help.

Finally, Coretta handed over her sack to Jeremiah Wilson so he could weigh it. Jeremiah thought he was really important, Coretta could tell, now that he no longer had to work in the fields.

"Here you are, Miss Coretta," Jeremiah said. He handed Coretta a dirty envelope. "You're a mighty rich young lady now."

Coretta looked inside, counted the coins, and then said, "Not yet, Jeremiah, but I will be one of these days!"

The field where she had been pulling bolls was about five miles from her house, but Coretta knew a shortcut through the countryside, even if it meant being chased by a couple of dogs and having white women shout

at her. She didn't care. She just wanted to get home as fast as she could.

Just as Coretta reached one of the crossroads, though, she saw her father's truck pass, with a police car following closely behind. Coretta felt a chill go through her. Several times in the last year, Coretta knew that white men had falsely accused her father of breaking all kinds of laws. The police had even stopped him on numerous occasions for questioning. Coretta had heard stories about what the police in Perry County did when they pulled black people over. So far, they'd done nothing but talk to her father, and she hoped this was all that had happened today.

Coretta waited until both vehicles were out of sight before she crossed the road to the next field and starting running toward her house.

When Coretta finally came in sight of her front yard, she saw her father's truck parked in the drive, and she breathed a sigh of relief. Still, she wondered what had happened.

Coretta's parents were sitting in the swing on the front porch when Coretta came into the yard. "Hi, Mama! Hi, Daddy!" she said, as pleasantly as she could. "How was your day?"

"Fine, sweetheart," Mr. Scott said. "How was *your* day?"

"Fine too," Coretta said. "I got paid." She showed them the envelope. "So far I've made four dollars, and I'm hoping to have at least eight by the time all of the cotton has been picked."

"That's wonderful, sweetheart," Mrs. Scott said. "We're mighty proud of you."

When her parents just continued to smile at her without saying anything else, Coretta knew that she would not learn from them what had happened, so she went on into the house, where Edythe was setting the table and Obie Leonard was reading a book.

"Why aren't you helping?" Coretta asked him as she washed her hands. "How many times have you heard Daddy say he won't have lazy people in his house?"

Obie Leonard stood up reluctantly, washed his hands, and said, "What do you want me to do?"

Coretta sighed, then said, "Just sit back down and stay out of the way."

Obie Leonard sat back down and opened his book again.

Coretta whispered to Edythe what she had seen earlier.

"So that's why Daddy put a gun in the glove compartment of his truck," Edythe said.

"He did?" Coretta said.

Edythe nodded. "He told Mama that a policeman stopped him and asked him why he had threatened a couple of white men in town," she said, "and Daddy told him that it was the other way around, that the two white men had threatened him because he was taking away their business."

"What business?" Coretta asked.

"They have trucks too, and they haul lumber when they can get the work," Edythe said, "but they told Daddy that he was taking their jobs away."

"Daddy has just as much right to haul that lumber as they do," Coretta said angrily.

"Well, they're *white*, Coretta," Edythe said, "so they don't exactly feel the same way you and I do."

For the next several weeks, Coretta worried every day that her father wouldn't come home after work, that he'd pull out his gun, and then a white man would shoot him. She knew that there was no way her father would use it on another person, because he wasn't that kind of man.

One day, just as they got home from school, Coretta noticed that their father's truck had a dented fender, and she wondered what had happened to cause it.

Coretta raced into the house, followed by

71

Edythe and Obie Leonard. Mr. Scott was sitting at the kitchen table, his head in his hands, and Mrs. Scott was standing over him, telling him that everything was going to be all right.

"What's wrong?" Coretta said.

"Nothing, children, nothing," Mrs. Scott said. "It's all right."

Mr. Scott raised his head. "They need to know, Bernice," he said. "It could affect us all."

Earlier, Mr. Scott and Mr. Thomas had been involved in a collision. Mr. Scott was sure it had been Mr. Thomas's fault, that he had ignored a stop sign, but the only witnesses were Mr. Scott, Mr. Thomas, and two of his helpers. Mr. Thomas had been knocked unconscious and was now in the hospital.

"If he dies, they'll put your father in prison," Mrs. Scott said. "He'll never get a fair trial."

Coretta couldn't believe it. Why would

something like this happen to them? They couldn't put her father in prison! It would destroy the family.

For the next week, Coretta couldn't keep her mind on anything but the accident. Several times at school, her teacher had to tell her to pay attention. At meals, she could hardly eat, and at night, she could hardly sleep.

Finally, one day when they got home from school, Mrs. Scott said, "Mr. Thomas is going to be all right. He's not even going to bring charges against your father."

That evening, Coretta made up for the meals she had missed, and once her head hit the pillow that night, she was instantly asleep.

Good news suddenly seemed to be the order of the day when, one evening, Mr. Scott announced that he was out of debt. He had finally been able to pay off all he owed Mr. Thomas for his truck and for all the charges the family had made at the mercantile store.

"Starting tomorrow," Mr. Scott announced, "I'll be working for myself, and every cent I make, I can keep and save it for our new house."

By the next month, though, the new house had moved farther down the list of things to buy.

One evening, Mr. Scott came home and said, "I've decided to buy Mr. Jackson's old sawmill, fix it up, and go into business for myself."

"Oh, Daddy, that's wonderful," Coretta said. "You'll be the owner, so nobody can tell you what to do!"

But Mrs. Scott said, "Obie, we've passed by that place many times, and it's not in very good condition. Are you sure you're doing the right thing?"

"Of course, he's doing the right thing,

Mama," Coretta said. "With Daddy in charge, it'll soon be the biggest and best sawmill in this part of Alabama."

"Well, I don't know about that," Mr. Scott said, "but if we all help out, then it'll be up and running at full capacity in the next couple of weeks."

Whenever they could, the entire Scott family all worked together to get the old mill in good operating condition. Even some of the white men in the area who knew they could trust Mr. Scott more than they could trust the white mill owners offered the family their services. Finally, the mill was ready to receive hauls from loggers felling trees all over that part of western Alabama.

As often as she could, Coretta helped out, writing down who delivered what and how much her father would charge to mill the logs. Soon, though, she began to detect hostility on the part of the two white workers who had stayed on at the mill after her father had bought it.

One evening, as Coretta rode home with her father from the mill, Mr. Scott said, "Joe came by to see me today. He wanted to make me an offer."

Coretta knew that Joe was the one worker who always seemed angry about one thing or another and was constantly complaining to her father about how things were done at the mill.

"What kind of an offer?" Coretta asked.

"He wants to buy the mill from me," Mr. Scott said. "I told him I didn't want to sell it."

"What did he say to that?" Coretta asked.

"He more or less told me I'd be sorry," Mr. Scott said.

It worried Coretta to hear this, but she kept it to herself.

Sure enough, two weeks later, when Coretta and Mr. Scott drove to the sawmill one Saturday morning, the entire operation had been reduced to ashes, not only the building and equipment that Mr. Scott owned but also the piles of logs that loggers had brought to be milled.

As Coretta and her father stood there, taking in the damage, a couple of white men drove up. They were two of the ones who had originally helped Mr. Scott get the mill running again.

"You need to report this, Obie," one of the men said. "You need to ask for an investigation."

"You do, Obie," the other man said. "There's no way this wasn't deliberately set, and you need to get to the bottom of it."

Mr. Scott nodded, but after the two men had left, he said to Coretta, "It wouldn't make any difference if I did, because I'm a black man, and white people think I shouldn't have my own business, anyway, because I'm supposed to work for them all my life. No black man should ever rise above 'his place.'"

"Daddy, that's not true!" Coretta cried. "That's just not true."

That next week, Mr. Scott went back to hauling lumber for other mill owners, who took him on without ever asking him what had happened to his own mill.

The New House

Over the next few months, the only thing on Coretta's mind was getting even with the white men who had destroyed her family's sawmill. She thought about it during the day, and she dreamed about it at night.

"Why aren't *you* angry, Daddy?" Coretta demanded of him one evening, after she realized that her father had never again mentioned what had happened. "Why aren't you really angry and coming up with ways to punish them?"

"Coretta Scott, I'm disappointed in you if you think that's the kind of person your father is," Mr. Scott said. "I have better things to do with my life, daughter, than to sit around thinking about evil all the time."

Coretta just looked at her father as he went back to reading the Bible. He was such an amazing person. He never seemed bitter about anything, despite all of the things that had happened to set him back, after all the harassment by white people who didn't think black people had a right to achieve more than they, themselves, achieved, no matter how hard the black people worked.

Suddenly, Coretta realized what all this was doing to her. She was becoming bitter and angry and ugly. At that moment, she made a decision to try to temper her feelings. She knew it would be hard, very hard, but she didn't want her life to be so empty that all she would have accomplished at its end would be thinking up ways to get even with white people for what they had done not only to her and her family but to *all* black people.

"You're right, Daddy, you're right, as always," Coretta said. "What I need to think about instead is what I can do to make changes in the system we live under."

Mr. Scott looked up. "Now, that's using your head, Coretta," he said, "and the first place to start is by getting a good education, so you'd better do your homework."

Coretta grinned back. "I finished it earlier," she said. "I actually wanted to."

"Well, now, this is a change for the better," Mr. Scott said. He returned her grin. "Things must be looking up for this family after all."

One day, in 1937, Mr. Scott came home and said, "I got us a new house! I got us a new house!"

"Praise the Lord," Mrs. Scott said. She sat down at the kitchen table. "I hate to admit this in front of you and the children, Obie, although I have already admitted it in front of the Lord, but I never thought this day would come."

"Oh, Mama!" Coretta said. "You should have had more faith!"

"I know, I know," Mrs. Scott said. "You're right, but I guess I had been so weakened by all the bad things that have happened to us, I let it cloud my mind."

"It doesn't matter now, Bernice, because we've all worked hard, saving our money, doing without some of the special things we wanted," Mr. Scott said. "And now in just a few days, we'll have a bigger house to live in."

That evening, Coretta wandered from the kitchen, into the bedroom, then back into the kitchen, then back into the bedroom, before she finally joined the rest of her family on the front porch.

"I had never noticed before how bare these wooden floors are," she said, "or how faded and peeling the wallpaper is."

Mr. Scott laughed. "That's because it was home, Coretta," he said, "and sometimes 'home' is more a state of mind than an actual physical presence."

"You're right, Daddy," Coretta said. "Until you told us we'd be moving into a new house, this really was 'home,' but now I've already started thinking of the new house as 'home' and this 'home' as just an old 'house.'"

"Coretta, you can be so confusing some-times," Obie Leonard said, looking up from the book he was trying to read in the fading light. "That just sounded like double-talk to me."

"I know what she meant," Mrs. Scott said. She sighed. "I'm excited about the move too, honestly, but this old house will always occupy a special place in my heart because there are so many wonderful memories attached to it."

"There are also some bad ones," Edythe said.

"I prefer to think only of the good ones,"

Mrs. Scott said. She stood up. "Well, I'm going to bed, because we have to get an early start in the morning."

Coretta looked first at her mother, then at her father. "Where are we going?" she asked.

"Into Marion, to a furniture store," Mr. Scott said. "We're going to buy all new furniture for our new house."

Coretta jumped up. "Do you mean it, Daddy?" she cried. "Do you really mean it?"

"I most certainly do," Mr. Scott said.

The next morning, everyone was up and dressed and ready to leave by the time the sun rose.

"We should go shopping for furniture every day," Mrs. Scott said. "I've never seen any of you so eager to get out of bed in the morning."

As they headed into town, Coretta watched the scenery pass by with a totally different eye. It wouldn't be long, she knew, until she would be traveling a different way, going wherever she was going. Although their new house was just a few miles away, it was down a new road.

When they got to Marion, Mr. Scott parked the truck in front of Anderson Brothers' Furniture Store, but then he noticed a sign that said the store wouldn't be open for business for another twenty minutes.

"Well, I don't want to sit in the truck," Coretta said. "I'm going to do some window shopping."

Coretta and Edythe climbed out of the back, jumped the high curb, and walked over to the show windows. In order to see all of the displays, they put their faces as close to the glass as possible and shielded their eyes with their hands.

"I love that bed over there, Coretta," Edythe said, "the one with those tall posts."

"Oh, I don't," Coretta said, "but I do like . . ." She stopped as a woman at the back of the store seem to be motioning for them to move away. Coretta mouthed the word "What?"

The woman, still at the rear of the store, was now gesturing angrily for them to get away from the window.

"We're going to buy some furniture," Coretta mouthed to the woman. "We're just looking until you open the door."

All of a sudden, the woman charged angrily through the store, opened the front door, and shouted, "I told you girls to get away from that window, because you're getting it dirty, sticking your noses up against it like that, and if I have to tell you . . ."

"Good morning, ma'am. We're here to buy some furniture for our new home."

Coretta and Edythe turned around. Their father was standing behind them, smiling at the woman.

"My daughters were looking through your show window, trying to decide what they wanted," Mr. Scott continued, "and I'm sure that they didn't mean to dirty it." He smiled

again. "Before we leave, after we've bought our furniture, if you'll give me a damp cloth, I'll wipe everything clean for you."

The woman pursed her lips and for just a moment seemed at a loss for words, but then she said, "That won't be necessary, but we don't give credit to colored folks, so I don't see how . . ."

"We don't need your credit, ma'am," Mr. Scott said, still smiling pleasantly. "We'll be paying cash."

"Well, then, I guess it'll be all right," the woman said. She took a watch out of her pocket, looked at it, and added, "I suppose it's close enough to opening time that if you'd like to come on inside and look around, well then, I guess that's all right too."

"We'd like to do that very much," Mr. Scott said pleasantly. He turned back toward the truck. "Bernice, Obie Leonard, come on."

For the next two hours the Scotts walked all around the store, trying to decide which pieces of furniture would be best for their new house. Each time Mr. and Mrs. Scott made the final decision on an item, always the largest piece available, with Mr. Scott assuring the family that that meant it was the sturdiest and would last the longest, one of the clerks would inevitably say, "That one's kind of expensive. Are you sure you can afford it?" and Mr. Scott would always reply, "Yes, I'm sure."

When Mr. Scott finally paid, no one at the store seemed happy, and some of the people even seemed a little angry that a black family could afford to buy furniture that even they couldn't. Although they kept their mouths closed, Coretta could tell from the looks on their faces exactly what they were thinking.

In the end, it took five trips in the truck to get the furniture to the new house, but there were family and friends waiting there, which made the unloading go faster.

Finally, all of the furniture was inside, and

arranged, at least for the time being, the way that Mrs. Scott wanted it.

That night at supper, Mr. Scott said, "At church tomorrow we need to give extra thanks to the Lord for our good fortune and we need to ask him to forgive us for all the unkind things we were thinking about the white folks who had to wait on us at the furniture store in Marion today."

"Amen," Coretta said, trying hard to stifle a giggle.

Coretta always enjoyed going to church every Sunday, even when it was hot inside and the minister's sermon never seemed to end. Not only did it make her feel good to ask God's forgiveness for all the mean thoughts that had filled her head during the week, mostly about white people, it was also the week's biggest social occasion.

Coretta knew it was probably a sin to spend any time wondering what her relatives and friends would be wearing to worship, but it was as if the tribulations of the weekdays had been thrown off and a person's best clothes represented being reborn.

"Hold still, Coretta, or I'll never get your hair braided," Mrs. Scott said. "You are just so wiggly this morning."

"I'm sorry, Mama, but I'm just so happy about our new house that I can hardly stand it," Coretta said. "Anyway, I'm old enough to braid my own hair, so you don't really have to."

"Well, I like fussing over you and Edythe on Sunday mornings," Mrs. Scott said, "so just let me have my chance while you're still at home."

This morning, they'd all be going in the truck, but sometimes, when Mr. Scott was working, they had to walk. When they did that, they made sure they were far enough away from the road that when white people drove by on their way to church, too much dust didn't get on their clothes.

After spending several minutes socializing with family and friends they hadn't seen since last Sunday, the Scotts all sat down together in the pew, which, while not formally assigned to them, was always where they sat.

The church pianist, Mrs. Garland, began pounding on the keys so loud that it sometimes hurt the ears of whoever was sitting close to her, but once the minister told them what they were going to sing, Coretta knew the voices of the congregation would soon drown her out.

"Amazing Grace, Brothers and Sisters," the minister shouted. "We'll begin our praise to our Lord with that fine old hymn."

As always happened, once the singing began, Coretta was transported out of Perry County. She wasn't sure exactly where, but she thought it was probably heaven, since she believed that only angel voices could sound this joyous. "Amazing grace, how sweet the sound," Coretta sang,

"That saved a wretch like me.
I once was lost, but now I am found,
Was blind, but now I see."

When the sermon began, Coretta was surprised that each word out of the minister's mouth meant something to her today. She didn't feel the need to yawn, she didn't feel the need to look around, and she didn't feel the need to continue singing over and over in her head the hymns they had just finished.

At the end of his message, when the minister said, "God loves us all, my friends, and I can tell you now that people, all people, not just white people, will reap what they sow. My message to you, then, is just keep on praying, especially for our brothers and sisters who are in pain today. Never forget, Brothers and Sisters, the Bible has the answers to all our questions, it teaches us what to do, and someday, someday, God will straighten things out."

"Amen!" Coretta said, a little louder than she had meant to, but she didn't add that God knew that if he ever needed any help from her, she would be available.

Another Warning

"You are going to get in a lot of trouble, that's what," ten-year-old Coretta said to Obie Leonard as they raced toward the front porch of their house. "How dare you tell your friends that I'd do their homework for them. Mrs. Forest heard you, and then she gave me a talking-to, telling me she was disappointed in what I was doing."

"I'm sorry, Coretta, I really am," Obie Leonard said. "I was bragging on how smart you are, honestly, so please don't tell Mama. You know what she'll do to me."

"That's why I'm going to tell her, Obie Leonard," Coretta said as they went into their house. "Maybe it'll teach you not to do that anymore."

"Here, here, what's wrong with you two?" Mrs. Scott said. "I knew you were coming when you were still a mile away."

Coretta looked at Obie Leonard, then took a deep breath and let it out. "Nothing, Mama," she said. "I was just fussing at Obie Leonard for being silly, that's all."

"Well, go get changed, and then wash up," Mrs. Scott said. "Supper is ready."

"Where's Daddy? Where's Edythe?" Coretta asked. "Why aren't we going to wait for them?"

"Your father's working late tonight. He's got a triple load of lumber to haul from Mr. Phillips's mill," Mrs. Scott said. "Edythe came in early from school because she wasn't feeling well, so she went into Marion with Mrs. Platte to get some medicine at the drugstore.

They're going to spend the night at Mrs. Platte's sister's house, and then Mrs. Platte is going to take her directly to school in the morning."

Coretta never liked it when her father worked late hauling logs from the sawmills, because they were deep in the forest, and the roads were narrow and scary. In fact, just that morning Coretta had overheard her father say again, as he always did, "I may not be back, Bernice, so if anything happens to me, you make sure the children finish school." Coretta knew he carried the gun in his glove compartment, but she still believed he would never use it, even if his life was threatened.

At the table, Coretta noticed that Obie Leonard was the only one who ate everything on his plate and even took second helpings. Her mother just sat and stared at the food. Coretta at least moved the helpings around.

Finally, Mrs. Scott said, "Well, let's get this cleaned up, and then I think I'm going to bed."

When they had finished in the kitchen, Obie Leonard went to his room and Coretta went to hers. The room that Coretta and Edythe shared was far enough away from their parents that when Coretta played the Victrola, it couldn't be heard if she kept the volume low enough, and now, with the plan she had conceived during supper, she wouldn't be heard leaving the house. Although her father had often been later than this coming in, Coretta just had a bad feeling about tonight, and she was going to find out if anything had happened to him. She knew the road her father would be taking, coming from Mr. Phillips's mill.

When Coretta thought that her mother might either already be asleep or at least getting drowsy, she put on her coat and quietly left the house. The sky was clear, and the moon was bright enough so that she could see her way on the road. From time to time she climbed over rail fences to cut through the woods, but she often had to feel her way from tree to tree.

Coretta tried not to think about what kinds of creatures might be hiding in the darkness, creatures that only came out at night, but several times the bright eyes of a skunk or a raccoon or a possum peered out at her from the underbrush.

Just as Coretta came to the edge of the woods, up to a fence that bordered the road, she thought she heard loud voices. As quietly as she could, she made her way toward the sounds.

Suddenly, Coretta stopped, almost afraid to breathe, in case she'd be heard. *My father's truck is parked in the middle of the road!* Coretta counted five other vehicles, three pickups and two automobiles, that had it surrounded.

Coretta crouched down, to where most of her body would be hidden by tall grass, and slowly edged her way to the rail fence.

"We've warned you time and time again, Obie," a man's voice said. Whoever he was, he was waving a long stick in front of her father's face. "You're taking our livelihood from us, boy, hauling all this timber in your truck, and we want it to stop."

"If it doesn't," a second man brandishing a gun said, "then we're going to kill you and throw your body into the swamp, where you'll never be found."

The other men started shouting, "Yeah! Yeah! That's what we're going to do, boy! We'll teach you to stay in your place and not be so uppity!"

They're going to kill him! Coretta thought. *They're going to kill my father right here before my eyes!*

Coretta knew there was only one thing to do. She'd scream at the top of her lungs so they'd know there would be a witness to the crime they were about to commit, and then maybe that would give her father a chance to escape into the woods and find his way back to their house.

Coretta opened her mouth, but before any sound could escape, she heard her father say, "Now, you men know that I haven't done anything wrong, and if you examine your hearts, you'll see that I'm only doing the best I can to make a living so I can support my family, too."

"You don't have the right to take work from us!" one of the men shouted.

Calmly, Mr. Scott said, "I'm not taking work from any of you." He waved his hand toward the side of the road. "There are trees everywhere, which means there is plenty of lumber, and there are plenty of mill owners who don't have enough drivers to take the lumber they mill to the lumberyards in this part of the state."

Coretta was astonished at what was taking place before her. Not once had her father bowed his head so that his eyes wouldn't be in direct contact with the white men's eyes, like so many black men and women did. Instead, he was looking straight at them, his head held high as he calmly explained to them why he had the right to do what he was doing.

"I've known you men all of my life," Mr. Scott continued, "and you know that I'm a God-fearing person who has never once caused any of you harm, and if you'll just let all of that anger out of your head, then you'll know I'm speaking the truth. These are hard times for everyone, and I understand that, but I'm not doing anything to make your life more difficult."

For several minutes none of the men said anything, and Coretta held her breath, expecting at any moment for one of them to lunge at her father.

Eventually, one of the men muttered something that Coretta couldn't make out and left the circle. He walked back to his pickup and drove off. Within minutes, the rest of the men left too, leaving Mr. Scott alone in the middle of the road. After the noise of the departing vehicles had died away, with only the chirping sounds of crickets and cicadas left, Coretta saw her father put his head in his hands and, from the shaking of his shoulders, could tell he was crying. Coretta wanted so much to go to him, but she knew he would be embarrassed and probably angry that she had left home so late, exposing herself to danger.

Finally, Mr. Scott got back inside his truck, shifted gears, and drove away. Immediately, Coretta started back toward their house, but this time she stayed off the road, thinking that if one of the men who had stopped her father suddenly changed his mind about not killing him and found her instead, she would probably be the one who ended up dead.

When Coretta got back to her house, she saw that her father's truck was parked outside. There was also a light on in her parents' bedroom.

This time, Coretta slipped back into the house through the window in her bedroom, then quietly made her way to the door of her parents' bedroom.

"But they let me go, Bernice, because I looked them in the eye and talked calmly to them," her father was saying.

"They may not do that next time, Obie," Mrs. Scott said. "How could I rear the children if you were gone?"

"You would survive, Bernice, I have no doubt about that," Mr. Scott said. "I can't give in to them—that's exactly what they're hoping for."

"Would that be so bad?" Mrs. Scott asked.

"Of course it would, Bernice," Mr. Scott said. "Why would you even want to live if you only lived in fear?"

After a few minutes, Mrs. Scott said, "You're right, Obie. You've always been right about this."

• • •

Mr. Scott didn't give in. He continued to haul logs and lumber for several mills, and he continued to receive threats against his life and against the lives of every member of his family.

Neither of her parents ever mentioned what had happened that night on the lonely road, and as much as she tried when she thought about it, Coretta could not contain her anger, no matter the promises she had made to herself, over and over.

"Why do white people treat us like this?" she would almost always ask at some point at supper. "Why don't they think we're as good as they are?"

Either her mother or her father would always reply, "You are as good as they are, Coretta, and if you get a good education, you'll be somebody, and nobody will ever be able to take that away from you."

Later, Coretta would decide that it was during the following weeks that she finally

106

decided that going to school really was the answer to how she could help the next generation of black Americans. One evening, in her room, she made a vow to get the best education she could, so she would be in a position to make sure no one else would have to endure what she and her family had.

We're Going to Lincoln High School

Eleven-year-old Coretta's first day in sixth grade, her final year at the all-black elementary school at Heiberger, started the way all the other school years had started. Rain or shine, she and Edythe and Obie Leonard would walk the three miles to school and back each day, hoping that the school buses carrying the white children to their school wouldn't splatter them with mud or cover them with the fine dust the wheels stirred up.

The faces of white children staring at them from the back windows, sticking out their tongues, had been burned into Coretta's mind. When Coretta shook her fist at them, she could tell it made them all very angry, because black people just didn't do things like that to white people, but Coretta didn't care. In fact, she enjoyed the feeling it gave her, even though she knew she wasn't doing what the Bible taught, that she should turn the other cheek.

That day, when Coretta saw their school in the distance, she remembered that it had once been just an unpainted wooden frame building, with one room, in which more than one hundred pupils crowded each school day. Now, it was divided into two rooms, separating the lower grades from the upper grades, and had even been painted inside and out.

"It is still not as nice as the school that the white children go to, though," Coretta muttered.

"And it never will be," Edythe said. She turned to Coretta. "I know what you're thinking, and you need to quit worrying so much about it. It's never ever going to change around here."

"Oh, yes it is," Coretta assured her. "Oh, yes it is!"

"*What's* going to change?" Obie Leonard asked her.

"Well, for one thing, we're going to have real blackboards to write on, not just wooden walls that have been painted black. And we're also going to have indoor toilets, not outhouses that smell so bad, you can hardly breathe when you pass them."

"And?" Edythe said.

"We're going to have real desks, made for schools, not wooden benches, or those rough things that Mr. Jones made and forgot to sand,

111

so that I get splinters in my legs every time I sit down in them."

"And?" Obie Leonard said.

"And we're going to have real textbooks, new ones, and our parents won't have to pay for them either, just like the parents of the white children don't, and we'll have a library, with other books that you don't have to read but that you'll want to read because they'll be books about all kinds of interesting things."

Coretta continued to list the changes that she planned to make so that the black children who attended this school after she was gone would get a better education.

"I hope they don't change teachers, though," Edythe said, "because no one could ever be as good as Mrs. Bennett."

"I know," Coretta said.

In fact, if it hadn't been for Mrs. Mattie Bennett, Coretta was sure that she would just have quit and started working full-time in the fields, given how angry she was for most of the years she attended classes at Heiberger. Mrs. Bennett had made sure that Coretta was able to channel her anger into doing well in her subjects so that she wouldn't drop out, as some of the other students had done over the years.

"I've been teaching a long, long time, Coretta," Mrs. Bennett had told her. "I can recognize talent when I see it. I think one of my jobs is to make sure that talented pupils know what God has given them and to help them to develop that talent to the fullest."

According to Mrs. Bennett, if Coretta failed to achieve what God had meant for her to achieve, then she would have committed an unpardonable sin, and Coretta had learned enough at church on Sundays to know the consequences of that.

That first day, when school was over and all of the children had started to leave the building,

Mrs. Bennett stopped Coretta. "I want to visit with you for a while, dear," Mrs. Bennett said. "When I'm ready to go, I'll take you home in my wagon."

Coretta asked Edythe if she'd mind walking home with Obie Leonard by herself, but Edythe grinned and said, "Who told you I was walking by myself? Arnold asked me if he could walk with us, and I told him he could."

Coretta grinned back. She didn't particularly think Arnold was much of a catch, but he was nice enough, and Edythe seemed to enjoy his silly jokes.

"Well, all right, then," Coretta said. "I'll see you later."

Mrs. Bennett had to explain a couple of math problems to the Carlton twins, while Coretta looked on from the back of the room. Coretta was amazed at Mrs. Bennett's clear reasoning, which helped Jody and Jordan see the light.

Finally, after everyone had left, Mrs. Bennett joined Coretta in one of the desks at the back of the room.

"I've always believed you were capable of learning almost anything, Coretta," Mrs. Bennett began, "but until recently you just didn't seem to understand what education could mean to your future."

"I guess I didn't, Mrs. Bennett," Coretta agreed, "but in the last few months, I've realized that we black people can only change the world if we are smart enough to know how."

"Well put, Coretta," Mrs. Bennett said. "Since the sixth grade is the highest grade here, that means for many of the students, it's the end of their schooling. But I don't think it's the end of education for you or Edythe."

"What do you mean?" Coretta asked.

"Well, just from talking with your parents at church, Coretta, I know that they want you both to continue your studies," Mrs. Bennett said, "and that would mean going to Lincoln High School in Marion."

Coretta knew that Lincoln High School was the nearest high school for black students, but Marion was more than ten miles away. There was no way she and Edythe could walk that distance to and from the school each day, no matter how much they wanted to. Still, she decided not to interject anything negative into the conversation—it was part of her recent decision to always be as positive as she could about everything in her life.

"We'd love to do that, Mrs. Bennett," Coretta said. "I know that Lincoln High School has a good reputation."

Coretta knew that part of the reputation was due to the fact that almost half of the teachers there were white people from the northern states. Often, black teachers had only gone to college for one or two years before they were allowed to teach. Coretta was sure that they

116

all tried as hard as they could and did the best job they could, but they weren't always very far ahead of some of the students they were trying to teach.

"I have a plan, Coretta," Mrs. Bennett said. "During this next year, besides learning new things, you and I are going to fill in the holes from your first five years."

"*Holes?*" Coretta said.

Mrs. Bennett nodded. "You yourself know that in the beginning, unlike Edythe, you didn't apply yourself, and when you enter Lincoln next year, I don't want anyone thinking that you shouldn't be there."

"Yes, ma'am," Coretta said. She didn't dare even to think that there was a possibility of her doing so, but she knew it wouldn't hurt to dream about it for the next year. "Yes, ma'am," she repeated.

True to her word, Mrs. Bennett worked with Coretta during and after school, making sure she remembered her math, her spelling, her history, and her English from the last five years and then introducing the material she needed to pass the sixth grade. It didn't take long before Mrs. Bennett was sure that all of the holes had been filled in. But Mrs. Bennett also started lending Coretta books from her own library, which she called the classics of American and British literature.

Coretta enjoyed her music lessons the most. Whenever the school had special programs, Coretta was always asked to sing a solo. In the small classroom, with people standing so close together, Coretta stood under the dim spotlight of a kerosene lamp. For a while, Coretta was no longer in western Alabama but in one of the world's great music halls, and people had paid to come hear her. When Coretta finished singing, for just a few seconds, there was a hush over the audience. People marveled at the performance and didn't want it to end. Then they burst into applause, and Coretta bowed graciously before them.

It was after one such performance, which the Scott family all attended, that Mr. Scott announced to both Coretta and Edythe, "Come fall, you'll both be attending Lincoln High School."

Something Terrible Has Happened

"Daddy, Mama," Coretta said. "How will we get there?"

"We can't walk ten miles there and back every day," Edythe chimed in. "I want to go to high school more than anything else in the world, but I'd always be so tired, I'd probably fall asleep in class."

Mr. Scott smiled. "We'll explain everything to you girls when we get home," he said.

On the ride back to their house, Coretta and Edythe lay down in the bed of the truck and looked up at the stars.

"How many do you think there are, Edythe?" Coretta said.

"I don't know," Edythe said.

"Well, take a guess," Coretta said.

"All right," Edythe said. "I'd guess there are about a trillion trillion trillion, at least."

"I'm sure that's not even close," Coretta said, "although I've never really seen a number."

"Why did you want to know, anyway?" Edythe asked her.

"I was just thinking that, out of all those stars, however many there are, each of us has one of them that's a *lucky* star," Coretta said, "and I'm hoping that one right there, the one I'm pointing to right now, is mine."

"Why that one?" Edythe asked.

"That's one's always winking at me, that's why," Coretta said.

Edythe giggled. "Oh, Coretta, just a few minutes ago I was really looking forward to all the things we usually do in the summer," she said, "but now I can hardly wait until school starts again in September."

"Me too," Coretta said.

"Your mother and I have arranged for you to live in Marion," Mr. Scott said, when they got back home and were seated around the kitchen table. "We met a new couple at church, and the woman's sister and her husband, Louise and Abraham Franklin, live in Marion and have an extra room. They've agreed to rent it to us so that you girls will have a place to stay while you're at Lincoln High School."

"Won't that be expensive?" Coretta asked.

Mr. Scott shook his head. "I've been saving my barbering money just for this, Coretta," he said, "and I'm planning on taking on more customers in the fall."

"This is what we want for you girls," Mrs. Scott added. "You know how we feel about your getting a good education."

Coretta jumped up and hugged first her father's neck, then her mother's, and said, "Edythe and I couldn't have asked for better parents. We've been blessed, that's for sure."

"Well, we've been blessed by you, too, dears," Mr. Scott said. "This is a really exciting time in our lives."

Later that night, though, Coretta found her happiness somewhat diminished by thoughts of black families who had to sacrifice because the people who were in charge of the county's school system didn't see the need to use their buses to take black students to the high school in Marion. As far as they were concerned, it was perfectly all right if black education stopped at the sixth grade. "What do blacks need with an education, anyway?" Coretta had often heard white people say. "It doesn't take a lot of book learning to know how to clean houses."

"Stop it, stop it!" Coretta whispered to herself. Thinking about this was getting her so riled up that she wouldn't be able to go to sleep. Instead, she decided, she'd say a prayer to the Good Lord for blessing her and Edythe with parents who cared so much about them. She, in her turn, would make sure she did well so that Obie Leonard, who was still in elementary school, would be able to go to Lincoln High School when *he* was old enough.

Coretta was surprised at how fast summer went. She even enjoyed it, which she hadn't thought she would, being so ready as she was to begin her high school classes. There were large family picnics, swimming in the cool forest streams, and even trips to Marion to shop for material for new dresses. One of the times the Scotts were there, they went by the house where Edythe and Coretta would be living. It was only four blocks from the high school. Coretta immediately liked Mr. and Mrs. Franklin.

"This is like a dream," Coretta said.

"Let me show you your room," Louise said to Coretta and Edythe.

Everyone followed Louise through the house to a high-ceilinged room, twice the size of theirs at home, and right next to, Coretta had noticed, a large bathroom.

"This is heavenly," Edythe said as she peered inside. "It's so big."

"Well, this will be your home for the four years you're at Lincoln," Louise told them. "Abraham and I hope you'll be happy." She sniffed. "It'll be wonderful to hear girls' voices in this house again. Since our Magdalene and Tiffany moved up north to Chicago, it's been lonely around here."

Mr. Scott laughed. "You may be wishing for some quiet times, after our girls have been here a few days," he said.

"Oh, Daddy, you make us sound terrible," Coretta said.

"I'm just telling the truth, that's all," Mr. Scott said.

Louise laughed. "Don't worry," she assured them. "We're prepared for anything!"

In late August, the Scotts had a visit from two of the white teachers at Lincoln High School. Coretta was sitting on the porch one afternoon, when an old car pulled up in front of their house and two white people, a man and a woman, got out, smiled at her, and said hello.

"Hello," Coretta said. At first she thought it was somebody coming to complain about something her family was doing, something that only white people should be doing, but the man said, "I'm Robert Dishman. I teach English at Lincoln."

The woman offered her hand to Coretta and said, "I'm Julie Caruthers, and I teach drama at Lincoln."

126

Coretta said, "It's nice to meet you."

For a minute, Coretta didn't know what else to say. But Robert broke the silence with, "We've heard wonderful things about you and your sister, what great students you are. We just wanted to come out and introduce ourselves and see if you had any questions."

"I don't know," Coretta said. "I'm not sure what I should ask."

"Well," Julie said, "if you and Edythe have the time, we'll just tell you all about what you'll be doing at Lincoln."

"Oh, we'd love that," Coretta said. "Won't you please come inside?"

Robert and Julie ended up staying for dinner and didn't leave until almost ten o'clock. Before, during, and after the meal, the Scotts learned that Lincoln High School had begun as a private school, shortly after the Civil War, when there were no schools for black people in the South. It was started by the American Missionary Association, which sent white

127

missionaries down south to teach the children of former slaves.

"Of course, there were many white people who despised them," Robert said, "not only for teaching black children but also for living together with the black teachers in dormitories."

"Actually," Julie added, "many of them still do."

Mrs. Scott looked concerned. "Will our daughters be in danger?" she asked.

"There will always be mean people in the world, Mrs. Scott, and there may be some people in Marion who'll say ugly things," Robert said, "but we've never had any problems with anyone threatening individual students."

"We not only teach our students," Julie added, "we take care of them too."

When classes started at Lincoln High School that September, a whole new world opened up to twelve-year-old Coretta. From the moment she walked through the front door of the building, she felt as though she'd been transported in a time machine to one of the most marvelous places on earth.

That night, lying on their beds in their room at the Franklins', Coretta and Edythe shared everything that had happened to them.

"I talked to Mrs. Thomas today," Coretta said. "She's going to teach me how to play the trumpet."

"Do you want to play the trumpet?" Edythe asked.

"Well, I thought it would be good to have a skill once I get to heaven," Coretta said, "just in case the Angel Gabriel gets tired of tooting his own horn."

Edythe almost rolled off the bed, laughing, and then said, "Well, if lightning doesn't strike you in the next few minutes, sister, then I guess it's a good idea."

"And Miss Olive J. Williams, who graduated from Howard University, in Washington,

D.C., asked me to be in her singing group," Coretta said, "and we're going to start rehearsing for Handel's *Messiah* in a couple of days."

"Oh, Coretta, that's wonderful," Edythe said. She let out a contented sigh. "You know something? I doubt if there is even a *white* school in the South doing something like that."

"Well, honestly, Edythe, it makes no difference to me," Coretta said. "After just one day, I know for sure that Lincoln High School is as good as if not better than most of the other white schools around."

Coretta discovered that there was a lot of work involved in putting on a serious musical performance. All of the students had to learn to read the music, something that Coretta, who had always sung "by ear," was happy to do.

"You're amazing, Coretta," Miss Williams said several times a day. "You're going to be a brilliant artist."

"Thank you, Miss Williams," Coretta said. She tried to remain humble, but such praise coming from someone as accomplished as Miss Williams made it difficult.

The night of the *Messiah* performance, the auditorium was packed. Mrs. and Mrs. Scott and Obie Leonard were there, seated next to Edythe, and so were several other members of their church. There was also a sprinkling of white people, not only from Marion but from Birmingham, who had come, Coretta learned later, to hear the voice of this new soprano. At the end of the night, the choir received a standing ovation.

During the next few months, Coretta blossomed even more. She did well in all of her studies, but she did the best in music. She knew she had found her true calling. In every program that Miss Williams presented, Coretta either performed solo or sang with the chorus.

Coretta also learned to play the piano. She learned the songs from the classical repertoire as well as hymns, gospel songs, and spirituals. At their church in Marion, Coretta led the junior choir. When they performed, every seat in the building was occupied.

Over the next two years, Coretta and Edythe found that there simply wasn't enough time to learn all of the things they wanted to learn. If Coretta thought about that too much, she would get angry knowing that she had been denied all this information when she was younger. Still, those moments of anger became more and more fleeting—except when she and Edythe walked to school. Even with only four blocks between where they lived and Lincoln High School, there were times when white students harassed them.

One November morning in 1942, Coretta and Edythe headed toward school. They were later than usual because Coretta had forgotten to wind the alarm clock. Along the way they saw five white girls walking toward them, arms linked, laughing and chattering.

"Uh-oh," Edythe whispered. "Trouble ahead."

"Not for us," Coretta whispered back. She linked arms with Edythe and added, "They're not going to knock *me* off the sidewalk."

As the two groups got closer, Coretta could see that a couple of the girls had stopped laughing and were now giving them hostile stares.

"We're not doing what they expect us to do," Coretta whispered, "moving out of the way so they can pass."

When the two groups finally reached each other, they stopped, face-to-face and, for a minute no one said anything, then the girl in the middle said, "You'd better get off our sidewalk and let us pass!"

Coretta looked down at the sidewalk, then back up at the girl, and said, "I don't see your name down there. In fact, I don't see *any-one's* name down there," she said.

All five of the white girls started screaming and calling Coretta and Edythe nasty names. Coretta and Edythe just listened to them calmly, not once even blinking their eyes. When the girls finally ran out of steam, Coretta said, "Well, you've gotten that out of your system, so I guess you feel better. If you'll just move aside, then we'll be on our way."

"Yes, we have more important things to do than listen to five silly white girls," Edythe added.

"You just wait!" one of the girls screamed as she moved off the sidewalk. "When my daddy hears about this, he's going to . . ."

"Now, Edythe, in Shakespeare's play *Othello*, how would you explain Iago's malicious conduct?" Coretta asked, knowing that she was showing off.

"Well, Coretta, it is, of course, open to many

interpretations, but we have to remember what Iago, himself, said, as he was being led away: 'Demand me nothing: what you know, you know: / From this time forth I never will speak . . .'" Edythe stopped, turned to the five girls, and said, "But what about you? What do *you* think about Iago?"

One girl stuck out her tongue and made a face. Then the five of them wheeled around and continued down the sidewalk, huddled together.

"We shouldn't have done that," Coretta said as they continued on their way. "We really shouldn't have."

"Shouldn't have done *what*?" Edythe asked.

"Stooped to their level," Coretta answered. "We were brought up better than that."

Edythe sighed. "I know," she said. "Let's work on it, all right?"

Coretta nodded.

• • •

Things did seem to get better in the next few days, but on Thanksgiving night, that all changed. While Coretta, Edythe, and the Franklins were sitting around the fire, listening to the radio, the doorbell rang. It was Hampton D. Lee, an undertaker from Heiberger.

"Something terrible has happened, girls," he said when he saw Coretta and Edythe.

How Do People Like That Sleep at Night?

Coretta's heart was almost in her throat. *"What?"* she cried. *"What?"*

"Your house burned down," Mr. Lee said. "It's all gone."

"Are Mama and Daddy and Obie Leonard all right?" Edythe said. "Nothing happened to them, did it?"

"They're as fine as can be expected," Mr.

Lee said. "They're staying at your Grandpa McMurry's now."

Coretta looked at Edythe. "We have to go to them," she said. "We can't just stay here."

"I can drive you, if you want," Mr. Lee said. "I was going back to Heiberger tonight, anyway."

"That would be kind of you, Mr. Lee," Coretta said. "Just give us a few minutes to pack a suitcase."

The trip seemed to take forever, but they finally arrived at their grandfather's house, and Coretta and Edythe rushed inside while Mr. Lee followed with their suitcases.

The first thing that Coretta noticed was that her mother's eyes were red-rimmed, and she knew she had probably been crying ever since the fire.

"You girls didn't have to come," Mrs. Scott said, surprised. "You should have stayed in

Marion so you wouldn't miss school."

"It's all right, Mama," Coretta said. "We can make up any work we miss."

"Louise is going to tell our teachers what happened," Edythe added. "They'll understand, and I'm sure they'll think we did the right thing."

The next morning, as Mr. Scott started to leave the house, Coretta said, "Do you want me to go with you, Daddy?"

"Now, exactly where is it that you think I'm going, sweetheart?" Mr. Scott asked.

"I thought you were going to our house, I guess," Coretta said. "I thought that maybe in the daylight we could figure out how the fire started."

Mr. Scott shook his head. "Coretta, I think I know how the fire started, and I know for sure that there's nothing we can do about it except start over. That's why I'm going on to work, sweetheart, so that we can start over."

Coretta watched her father get into his truck and drive away. She wondered how many other mornings in his life he had done the same thing, after one setback or another, knowing that it probably wouldn't be the last time.

"It's wrong! It's wrong!" Coretta shouted, tears now streaming down her face. "We shouldn't have to live like this. We shouldn't!"

Edythe and Mrs. Scott came into the living room just as Coretta started sobbing uncontrollably.

Mrs. Scott took Coretta in her arms and said, "I think I've cried enough for both of us, daughter, but I guess it won't hurt if you cry some yourself. It might help get some of the anger out of your system. Just remember this: No matter how hard it is for us to understand, the Good Lord knows what's going on. He has a plan for us."

Coretta looked up into her mother's eyes.

"It's just so hard, Mama," she said. "I try, I really do. But I have bad thoughts about white people sometimes, even though I know the Lord doesn't want me to." She started sobbing again and couldn't continue.

"Hush now, hush now," Mrs. Scott said softly.

When Coretta leaned her head on her mother's shoulder, a sense of calm filled her entire body the way it always had. After a few minutes, Coretta was no longer sobbing.

"I want to go there, Mama," Edythe said. "I want to see what they did."

At first, Mrs. Scott hesitated, then she said, "All right. We'll take one of your father's other trucks."

On the way to their house, Mrs. Scott told them that their father had been having more troubles too, while they had been in Marion.

"He now owns three trucks in all, girls, and that's three more than a lot of the white folks around here have," Mrs. Scott said. "While your father has prospered, those poor whites have gotten angrier and angrier about it. If they're not harassing him, they're telling lies about him to the police, trying to get him in trouble."

"I don't think I'll ever understand that, Mama, no matter how long I live," Coretta said. "Instead of wasting their time blaming Daddy for all their problems, why don't they work as hard as he works?"

"Oh, Coretta!" Edythe suddenly cried.

Coretta turned toward where Edythe was looking and saw nothing but blackened timber, some of it still smoldering, where their wonderful house had once stood. She choked back a sob. As her mother pulled into the driveway, Coretta closed her eyes, praying that when she opened them again, it would all have been a terrible dream and the house would be exactly as she and Edythe had left it when they moved to Marion.

Of course, it wasn't. When Coretta got

out of the truck and approached the ruins, she knew she could no longer pretend that it wasn't so bad. There was nothing left.

For a few minutes the three of them just stood silently, then Mrs. Scott said, "Your father, ever the optimist, said we'd rebuild. We can do that, but I can't stop thinking about the pictures of our family that we can never replace and of the gifts that had so much love when we received them."

Finally, Coretta turned to her mother and said, "We're going to find out who did this, and when we do, they're going to jail."

"Coretta," Mrs. Scott said. "You can't start blaming other people until we find out for sure."

"Mama, this was no accident," Coretta said.

"There could have been a spark from the chimney that landed on the—" Mrs. Scott tried to say, but Coretta stopped her with, "White people did this to us! I know they did!

It wasn't some spark from a chimney fire, Mama!"

Against their parents' wishes, Coretta and Edythe stayed home from school that next week. They were bound and determined to find out how the fire had started. The first thing they did was start questioning the people who lived around them.

"Did you see anyone suspicious around our house on the night of the fire?"

"Were there any cars or trucks that you didn't recognize as belonging to people around here?"

"Have you heard anyone talking about who might have done this?"

They asked every question that came to mind, but no one wanted to talk to them.

Finally, one evening, Coretta said, "Well, tomorrow, I'm going to talk to the fire chief in Heiberger and insist that he investigate."

"Coretta, it won't do any good," Mr. Scott

said. "In fact, it could do more harm by stirring up even more resentment toward us."

"It's hard for me to explain, Daddy, honestly, but these past few years at Lincoln High School have changed me, and I hope for the better," Coretta said. "People I trust, people who have my best interest at heart have shown me that I am just as good as anybody else around here, and I plan to stand up for all these injustices that are inflicted on us."

Mr. and Mrs. Scott just looked at each other, and Coretta knew they wouldn't try to stop her. After all, she was doing exactly what they really wanted her to do: break the bonds of slavery that still existed in the South.

That afternoon, Coretta and Edythe met with the Heiberger fire chief, who told them that he had already investigated the fire and that he had determined that it was an accident.

"But—," Coretta started to say, only to be stopped by, "Now, if you girls will clear out of here, I have more important things to attend to."

Coretta bit down on her tongue so hard that it was bleeding when they left the man's office.

"He was lying through his teeth," Coretta said.

"Of course, he was, Coretta," Edythe said. "What did you think he would do?"

"How do people like that sleep at night?" Coretta said.

"Soundly, I'm sure, because they don't believe they're in the wrong," Edythe said.

Two days later, Mr. Lee drove Coretta and Edythe back to Marion. By the time they arrived, Coretta had already decided that if she gave in to her anger about the fire, it would only play into the hands of the people who were in the wrong. What she had to remember, and what she knew she would have to remind herself of time and time again, was that education was the key. Eventually, people all over the country would listen to her when she told them that they could no longer discriminate against black Americans.

Alone in Marion

Try as hard as she could, Coretta wasn't able to get rid of the anger inside her.

Edythe was still angry too, but for some reason, she had an easier time with it. Once they were back in Marion, surrounded by classmates and teachers at Lincoln High School, Edythe threw herself into practicing with the Lincoln School Little Chorus.

"Frances and Cecil Thomas are the directors," Edythe told Coretta. "They have all kinds of contacts with colleges, and well, I'm not supposed to say anything, but—"

"Then don't say it," Coretta snapped. "If you were told not to say it, then don't say it."

Edythe blinked in surprise. "All right, I won't," she said. "But if you were anybody else but my sister, I'd have snapped right back at you just like, well, just like *Coretta Scott* does to people."

That brought a smile to Coretta's face, and she apologized. "I still don't want you to tell me, if you're not supposed to, Edythe, but congratulations on whatever it is."

"Thank you," Edythe said.

Coretta's anger about the fire began to manifest itself quite frequently. Wherever she went, she confronted anyone who, in walking toward her, seemed prepared to push her off the sidewalk.

From a few feet away, Coretta would say in a loud voice, "Please do not try to do what you're thinking you're going to do, because I am not going to move out of your way!"

The whites who Coretta knew had planned to do just that were so shocked by what they had just heard that they always stopped, with dropped mouths, and let her pass. Of course, after Coretta was on the other side of them, they usually muttered something mean about her. But Coretta decided that it was only because they were uneducated.

That spring, Edythe's choir went on a tour of colleges, black and white, around the upper Midwest. The last stop was Antioch College, in Yellow Springs, Ohio. The letter Edythe wrote Coretta from Yellow Springs arrived a week after the choir was back. When Louise handed it to Coretta, she opened it, but she didn't read it, letting Edythe do it instead.

"I found where I want to go to college, Coretta," Edythe said after she had finished the letter. "I have never felt so free in all my life."

• • •

The next year, Edythe graduated as valedictorian of her class. Since she was older than Coretta, she had been allowed to advance through some classes faster and to test out of others so she could be with students her own age. Coretta believed she could have done that too, but she never complained about it to anyone, certainly not to Edythe. She was thrilled for her.

That same week, a letter from Antioch College arrived at school, addressed to the principal, offering a year's scholarship, which included tuition and room and board, to any member of the Lincoln School Little Chorus, whose visit everyone at Antioch remembered so fondly. Although several students applied, Edythe won. She was overjoyed when the principal gave her the news. Edythe even asked the principal to read the letter several times, saying she hoped he wasn't just making it up.

On the way home that afternoon, Coretta

said, "Why would you think our principal made up something like that, Edythe?"

Edythe grinned. "Actually, I didn't really think it," she said. "I just wanted to hear over and over the part in the letter about how wonderful I was."

"Oh, you!" Coretta said.

In the summer of 1943, eighteen-year-old Edythe left for Ohio. For a while, Coretta felt all alone. She spent part of the summer with her family, who had moved into another house of their own, not too far from the one that had burned. Soon, though, she began to miss the intellectual stimulation of Lincoln High School, so she made arrangements to move back in with the Franklins for the summer. She even got a part-time job at the high school, helping to make sure everything there was ready for the coming fall.

Coretta was amazed at how much needed to be done, but it was wonderful being back among the books and the interesting conversations with the teachers.

Edythe's letters helped too. She told Coretta about the academic freedom at Antioch—about how you could say whatever you wanted and no one would threaten to run you out of town. Edythe was especially impressed that the college used the honor system, not only with housing, but with exams, holding each student responsible for his or her actions. Edythe always closed her letters with, "Coretta, you'd love it here!"

Coretta didn't have to be convinced. She was sure she would too. Now, all Coretta could think of was leaving for Yellow Springs, Ohio. She discussed her plans with her teachers, and they said they would write letters of recommendation for her.

When Coretta did go home on weekends, she also discussed her plans for college with her parents, and they told her they would try to help her as much as they possibly could.

They were sending money each month to Edythe, though, and they weren't exactly sure how much more they could afford.

"We'll just have to think of a way to make more money," Mr. Scott said.

"Oh, Daddy, you already work more than you should," Coretta said. "No, no, you're not going to add any more to your workload. I'll figure something out."

Back in Marion, Coretta learned that there was a white woman, a widow named Mrs. Roger Clooney, who was looking for a *colored girl* to do house cleaning, since her last *girl* had died a couple of weeks before.

"How old was this *girl* of hers?" Coretta asked. "A hundred?"

When neither Louise Franklin nor her friends seemed to understand, Coretta said, "That's what all whites call us women, no matter how old we are, *girls*. It makes me so angry, too."

"Well, Coretta, I'm not sure you and Mrs. Roger Clooney would get along very well," Louise said. "You should probably try to find something else to do."

"I can get along with anyone, if I have to, Louise," Coretta said, "and especially if I need the money." She took a deep breath and let it out. "Do you have Mrs. Clooney's address?"

The next day, after school, Coretta headed to Mrs. Clooney's instead of going home.

When Coretta rang the bell, Mrs. Clooney opened the door and let out a gasp. "What in the world are you doing on my front porch, girl?" she said in a true Southern accent. "You need to go around to the back door."

It was all Coretta could do to keep her mouth shut, but she said, "All right, Mrs. Clooney. I'll meet you there."

Mrs. Clooney seemed to blanch at Coretta's words, but she didn't say anything. Coretta went down the porch steps, around the side of the house, and through a trellised gate. She had to admit that Mrs. Clooney's backyard was beautifully landscaped. *Maybe working here won't be too bad,* Coretta decided, *if I can look out the windows from time to time.*

At the back door, Coretta knocked. It was opened by Mrs. Clooney, who honestly didn't see anything silly in what had just occurred.

For the next few minutes Mrs. Clooney went through a litany of what Coretta was expected to do. While Coretta thought the job was worth more than Mrs. Clooney was willing to pay, she didn't say anything, reminding herself constantly that this was merely a part-time job to earn enough money to leave the South.

Two weeks into the job, though, Coretta realized she had made a mistake. After several days of being forced to use the rear entrance, having to say "yes, ma'am" at least a hundred times while she was there, and having Mrs. Clooney always address her as "girl," Coretta had had enough.

157

"I won't be in tomorrow, Mrs. Clooney," Coretta said when it was time to leave. "I've decided I don't want to work here anymore."

"Well, girl, just where do you think you're going to work?" Mrs. Clooney said.

"Mrs. Clooney, my name is Coretta, Coretta Scott, not 'girl,'" Coretta said, "and I'm sorry your memory is fading so much that you can't remember that."

"Why, how dare you speak to me in that tone of voice!" Mrs. Clooney said.

"Good-bye, Mrs. Clooney," Coretta said, and turned to leave.

"Wait just a minute, you!" Mrs. Clooney shouted. "Where do you think you're going?"

"I'm going out the *front* door, Mrs. Clooney," Coretta said. "That's where I'm going."

All the way back to the Franklins' house, Coretta expected to be stopped by the police. She was sure that Mrs. Clooney had called them with some hysterical story about all the horrible things that her *colored girl* had done.

When she reached the Franklins' house, though, she hadn't seen a police car anywhere, and decided that Mrs. Clooney was still rooted in the same place, trying to figure out what the world was coming to.

For the rest of the summer, Coretta tried to get other jobs. But she realized that she would be facing some form of discrimination almost everywhere because of the color of her skin. She wouldn't tolerate that from anyone, she told herself. She just wouldn't.

Finally, school started. During the day, Coretta was able to lose herself in her studies. But at night, she lay awake for hours wondering how she would be able to go to college.

One afternoon in October, she got her answer. The principal had received another letter from the president of Antioch College. It wasn't an application for a scholarship that several students would have applied for—it was a scholarship offer specifically for *Coretta Scott*.

Coretta could hardly contain her joy. When she graduated in the spring, she would be going to Yellow Springs, Ohio, and a new life up north.

A Musical Career

With Edythe's having paved the way for her, Coretta didn't have a very difficult time adjusting to being so far away from home. At first, Coretta let Edythe speak for her on many occasions, and even allowed her sister to decide what to wear, what courses to take, what events to attend, and what people to be friends with. Before long, though, Coretta realized that she was living Edythe's life, not hers, so she began to make her own decisions about everything. Edythe's feelings weren't hurt at all—she adored Coretta, and Coretta adored her.

There were only two other black students in Coretta's freshman class at Antioch that fall. One of them was a young man whom everyone just automatically thought would escort Coretta to whatever dances or other events were held on campus. Coretta was astonished at this attitude. She thought the young man was nice, but she believed there should be more in common between two people than the color of their skin, so she never went out with him. There was a white student who shared her interest in music, though, and when he asked her out, she accepted.

At first, Coretta thought she'd continue her music studies, building on her success and reputation at Lincoln High School. However, being so far away from home had made her realize how difficult a career in music would be. Coretta decided to combine her love of music with the teaching profession, thinking that would give her a steady income.

When Coretta enrolled in the education program at Antioch, she learned that in order to receive her degree she would have to complete two years of practice teaching somewhere in the Yellow Springs area. Coretta looked forward to that. It would certainly add to her classroom skills.

For the first year, Coretta taught in the private elementary school that was on campus and was used as part of the teacher-training program. During the second year, though, Coretta was required to teach in one of Yellow Springs's elementary schools. Coretta already knew that Yellow Springs was integrated, unlike the schools in the South. White and black students attended classes together. She was looking forward to the experience because she had always believed that both races could learn to get along better if their children went to school with one another.

When Coretta applied to the Yellow Springs school board to teach at one of the schools in the district, though, her application was immediately turned down. She was shocked. When she asked why, she was told that even though the schools were integrated, all of the teachers in Yellow Springs were white. There were no plans to change that in the immediate future.

All of Coretta's dreams of a different life in a northern town began to disappear. While there might not be as much discrimination in this part of the country, she decided, it still existed. In many ways, Coretta thought it was worse: People pretended that everything was different, when it really wasn't.

Coretta complained to the president of Antioch. He sympathized, but he told her there was nothing he could do. Those decisions were not his to make. Instead, he offered Coretta the option of doing her second required year of practice teaching at the college's elementary school. When Coretta told the president that she didn't believe a second year in the same school would add that much to the experience she hoped to gain from practice teaching, he suggested that she apply to teach in Xenia, a nearby town. Xenia, the president explained, was still segregated, so he was sure she would have no problem finding a position in one of the black schools.

Coretta told the president in no uncertain terms that she had left Alabama to get away from segregated schools and that she would never return to one. She left the president's office, thinking she might find more support among the education faculty and students in her effort to teach in Yellow Springs, but no one seemed willing to join her in trying to get the members of the school board to change their minds. In order to finish her education degree, though, Coretta finally accepted the president's offer and did a second year of student teaching on campus.

Still, this incident had only steeled Coretta's will to change things. She became very active in Antioch's branch of the National Association for the Advancement of Colored People (NAACP). She also joined the Civil Liberties Committee and the Race Relations Committee. Coretta wanted people to know that if you told her she couldn't do something, she'd find a way.

At the same time Coretta was having so much trouble with the "education" part of her degree work, she was thoroughly enjoying her music courses. All of her professors, immensely impressed by her talent, encouraged her. Coretta's first public performance after coming to Antioch was in 1948, at a concert hall in the nearby town of Springfield. The audience's applause after her last solo tempered Coretta's anger somewhat at not being allowed to teach music in the public schools of Yellow Springs.

When Paul Robeson, a famous black singer

and Coretta's idol, came to Antioch to sing at a campus NAACP event, Coretta was asked to perform with him. The thought of being on the same stage with such a great man actually made her nauseated. Shortly before she was to sing she became so ill that she thought she would have to leave the auditorium. However, when she looked out into the audience at smiling black and white faces brought together by music, Coretta realized that she couldn't leave. If she did, she knew she would let everyone down.

That night, as Coretta took the stage, she felt that her family back in Alabama was with her in spirit. She also felt the presence of all the people who had suffered at the hands of others for no other reason than the color of their skin. Coretta knew it shouldn't be that way. She knew that she had, for some reason, been chosen to carry that message around the world.

She sang as though she had been possessed

by muses, and, after the performance she was cheered not only by the audience but by Paul Robeson himself. He told her that it would be a terrible sin for her to waste her vocal talents and that she should, no matter what the cost or hardships, seek out the best teachers in the world in order to fine-tune her talent.

Even though she was at a loss for words at the compliment, Coretta did finally manage a thank-you. She assured him that she would continue her training.

No matter how uncertain Coretta had been earlier, she knew that she was happiest when she was singing. So, in 1951, with graduation from Antioch approaching, she began applying to some of the best music schools around the nation, determined to become an opera singer. Coretta knew she had made the right decision when she received strong encouragement not only from her Antioch professors but from other students in the music program as well.

Coretta was admitted to several very prestigious schools, to her surprise. Although she wasn't offered any scholarships, Coretta finally chose to attend the New England Conservatory of Music, in Boston, Massachusetts.

A few weeks later, Coretta went home to Alabama and told her parents about her plans. They were both pleased—Mr. Scott even offered to pay her tuition—but Coretta, now twenty-four years old, had decided it was time for her to pay her own way. She could see how much her parents had aged while she was in Ohio, and she knew that they needed to be saving the money for a time when neither of them could work and for Obie Leonard, who was now attending Lincoln High School himself.

When it was time for Coretta to leave, Mr. and Mrs. Scott drove her to the railway station in Birmingham, where she boarded a train to Boston and took her seat in a coach car reserved for "colored people." It would be a long journey. Coretta knew she would have to change trains in Atlanta, then in Washington, D.C., and finally in New York, before the last leg to Boston, but it would also give her time to figure out exactly where her tuition money was going to come from.

Coretta was extremely tired by the time her train finally pulled into New York, but she was glad to have a few hours of lay-over before the train left for Boston. She decided to spend some of her money to telephone her parents. At the time, she did it just so she could hear their voices. But she received news that was the answer to all of her prayers: a letter from the Jessie Smith Noyes Foundation, offering Coretta a grant of $650 so she could continue her musical training. It had arrived in that day's mail.

As soon as Coretta arrived in Boston, she lost herself in her music studies. But even with the grant, it was difficult to make ends meet. The money she received covered her tuition, but it didn't cover her living expenses. The little money that she had saved up ran low quickly. Often, there were several days in a row when Coretta had nothing to eat and frequently, in the middle of a practice performance, in front of her instructors, she felt so faint, she wasn't sure if she could continue. Still, Coretta persevered, believing with all her heart that things would turn around. She had come too far to consider quitting, even if it meant several consecutive meals of peanut butter and graham crackers.

Finally, Coretta decided to have a talk with her landlady, Mrs. Bartol. She offered to clean Mrs. Bartol's house in exchange for her rent and a breakfast every morning. Mrs. Bartol, who was also a patron of Antioch College, accepted Coretta's offer. Although Coretta's schedule became even more hectic, her inner strength kept her going. She was doing what she had always dreamed of doing, and she could see a bright future for herself.

Coretta had only been in Boston for about six months when she received a telephone call from a black minister by the name of Martin Luther King Jr. They had a mutual friend, Martin told Coretta, a Mary Powell, who was also studying at the conservatory. Coretta smiled, knowing that Mary was very much a matchmaker. Martin told Coretta that Mary had thought the two of them might enjoy each other's company and that he was eager to meet her. Coretta told Martin that she thought it would be nice to meet him, too, but that right now, things were so hectic in her life, she didn't have much time to socialize. Still, she said, she hoped Martin would call her again sometime.

When Coretta saw Mary the next day, she told her about the telephone call, and for the next hour Mary told Coretta everything she knew about Martin. Coretta agreed that he really did sound like someone she would enjoy getting to know.

Soon, Coretta and Martin were talking on the telephone several times a week. Each time, after she had hung up, Coretta was amazed at how much she had enjoyed their conversation.

The next week, Martin invited Coretta to lunch, and she accepted. When Martin picked her up at the conservatory, though, Coretta was disappointed that he was much shorter than she had pictured him. Almost immediately, she felt ashamed that she had let a physical characteristic take on so much importance. Soon, just listening to what Martin had to say about every subject they discussed caused him to grow in stature in her eyes.

On their first date, Martin startled Coretta by telling her she had all the qualities he was looking for in a wife.

Coretta was flattered by such a compliment, but she made it quite clear to Martin that she planned to finish her studies at the conservatory and then move to New York to start her career in opera.

What Coretta didn't say, though she was thinking it, was that the last thing on her mind now was getting married.

Mrs. Martin Luther King Jr.

Martin persisted. He told Coretta that he'd never takc no for an answer. Coretta admired Martin—he had a strong belief in right and wrong—but she knew he would expect her to put home and family before a career. Coretta wasn't sure she was willing to do that.

One night, Coretta called Edythe, who was finishing up her degree at Ohio State

University, in Columbus. She told Edythe everything that had happened and asked her what she should do.

Without a moment's hesitation, Edythe told Coretta that she should marry Martin. That evening, Coretta decided that she would set aside any thought of becoming an opera singer and would say yes to Martin's proposal.

Coretta and Martin were married on June 18, 1953, on the front lawn of Coretta's parents' new home in Marion. She was now the wife of a minister.

Martin had devoured the works of some of history's greatest philosophers while studying for his advanced degrees. He read Aristotle, Thomas Hobbes, John Locke, John Stuart Mill, and Jean-Jacques Rousseau. But the person he admired the most, because of his nonviolent philosophy, was Mohandas—Mahatma—K. Gandhi, the man many considered to be responsible for India's independence. Martin wanted to emulate Gandhi's use of love and nonviolence to bring about change in the South.

After Martin finished his doctorate at Boston University, he was offered several positions in the north, both as a professor and as a pastor. However, he decided that he wanted to return to the South. He felt there was too much work to be done there. Coretta remembered how difficult it had been to grow up in the South, but supported her husband's decision nevertheless.

When Martin was called to the pastorate of the Dexter Avenue Baptist Church, in Montgomery, Alabama, he accepted. He and Coretta returned south to begin their life together.

Although the church was small, Martin started several outreach programs that soon attracted new members, and it wasn't long before blacks, both rich and poor, found themselves uplifted by their new minister's heartfelt messages.

Martin never rested. There were times when Coretta expressed concern about the toll his schedule was taking on his health, but Martin seemed incredibly happy with what he was doing. Coretta made sure that she was always there for him when he needed her, whether they visited the sick or counseled members and non-members of the church with personal problems. She even brought him late-night meals when he was working on difficult sermons.

At Coretta's urging, Martin joined the NAACP. Together, they became members of the Alabama Council on Human Relations. The goal of both organizations was to work for a better relationship between blacks and whites.

Much to Coretta's delight, the music minister at Dexter Avenue asked her to join the choir—not because she was the pastor's wife but because he had heard her sing and knew of her musical reputation at both Lincoln High

School and at Antioch College. Coretta was delighted. She had wanted to be a part of the choir since Martin had been named pastor, but she had waited to be asked, not wanting any of the members to think that she thought she was better than they were because of her musical background. It wasn't long before Coretta was being asked to sing at concerts given in cities all around the Montgomery area. She always accepted. Singing still brought joy to her.

On November 17, 1955, Martin and Coretta had their first child, a daughter, Yolanda Denise. Everyone in the family called her Yoki. Over the next few years the Kings welcomed three more children into their family: Martin Luther III, born on October 23, 1957; Dexter Scott, born on January 30, 1961; and Bernice Albertane, born on March 28, 1963.

During the early years of his ministry in Montgomery, Martin and Coretta became

good friends with the Reverend Ralph Abernathy and his wife, Juanita. Abernathy was the pastor of Montgomery's First Baptist Church, which gave the two men a common ministerial bond. Abernathy's children were also about the same age as the Kings', and a close friendship developed between them.

Martin loved his job, Coretta had close friends to spend time with, and they had a growing family. Coretta began to think that she would have a quiet life. Martin tried to bring about peaceful change in the South with the nonviolent teachings of Gandhi always at the back of his mind.

However, this was not meant to be. Not long after Yoki's birth, a black seamstress named Rosa Parks made a fateful decision while riding on a Montgomery bus that would forever change the United States.

In 1955, in Montgomery, Alabama, if black people wanted to ride city buses, they had to wait until white people boarded at the front, by the driver, paid their fares, and then took their seats in the front section. When every white person was aboard, black people were then allowed to board at the front and pay their fares, but they then had to get back off the bus and reboard at the rear door, so that they could sit in the back—*if there were seats available*.

If all the seats reserved for blacks were taken but there were empty seats for whites, blacks still had to stand in the aisles. If all the white seats were taken, though, a white person could demand that a black person stand up so the white person could sit down.

On December 1, Rosa Parks boarded a bus in downtown Montgomery for the ride home. She took a seat in the first aisle reserved for blacks right behind the last aisle reserved for whites. At each stop along the route, the bus got more and more crowded. Finally, at one stop, a white man boarded the bus and, seeing that there were no seats available to him in the white section, told Mrs. Parks to get up. She refused. The other black passengers stood, but Mrs. Parks remained seated. She was sick and tired of how the bus company treated black people day in and day out.

The bus driver pulled over to the curb and called the police. When they arrived, Mrs. Parks was handcuffed and taken to jail.

The next morning, Martin received a telephone call about Mrs. Parks's arrest. Blacks in Montgomery had decided to boycott the bus company. Without even considering the consequences, Martin invited organizers to meet at the Dexter Avenue Baptist Church. That evening, the church was full of angry people shouting that they had had enough. It was decided that, starting December 5, all black people would stay off the buses in Montgomery, that they would get to work and to school by other means.

Martin also asked taxi drivers, many of whom were black, to give special fares to people who were boycotting the buses. At home, Coretta received hundreds of telephone calls from both black and white people who offered to help with the problem of transportation.

The night before the boycott was to begin, Coretta and Martin stayed up all night talking. What if the boycott failed? If it did, it would set any movement toward equality back years, because whites would realize that no matter what they did, black people would accept it. Since there was a bus stop near where the Kings lived, Martin and Coretta decided at dawn to go see if any of the buses that stopped were carrying black passengers. If they weren't, that meant the boycott was working.

When the first bus rolled up to the stop, its

interior lights on, Martin and Coretta could tell that there were no black passengers on board. After three more buses had come by, all without any black people, the Kings knew that the boycott was succeeding.

That evening, in another meeting at the Dexter Avenue Baptist Church, Martin was elected to head the newly formed Montgomery Improvement Association (MIA), the whole purpose of which was to help black people who were participating in the bus boycott. By accepting the leadership, Martin knew that he was not only putting his own life in danger but the lives of his family, as well. When he informed Coretta of his decision, though, she told him in no uncertain terms that she supported his decision 100 percent.

Within a few days, Martin and some of the other members of the association met with bus company officials, and even Montgomery city officials, trying to get them to change their policies for black people. When they were unsuccessful, it was the unanimous decision of the MIA leadership to continue the bus boycott until the demands were met. More than fifty thousand black residents of Montgomery participated in the boycott.

On the morning of January 30, 1956, Coretta was at home visiting with a friend, Mary Lucy Williams, when she heard a loud noise in front of the house. Later, Coretta couldn't remember why it occurred to her to do it, but she shouted to Lucy that they needed to move to the back of the house. Within seconds, a loud explosion showered the living room with broken glass, covering the chairs where the two women had been sitting. Someone had thrown a bomb onto the porch. Although no one was hurt, the incident shook Coretta badly. She had no way of knowing then that this would be one of many such incidents in the years to come.

On November 13, 1956, the United States

Supreme Court ruled that segregated buses were unconstitutional, and the new law went into effect in Alabama on December 20, a little more than a year after the arrest of Rosa Parks. Now, black people sat where they wanted to on the buses in Montgomery, Birmingham, Memphis, and wherever else they had been told they couldn't.

Whites in Montgomery reacted violently to the new law. Many black homes and churches were bombed. Several sticks of dynamite were thrown onto the front porch of Martin and Coretta's house, but something was wrong with the fuses, so the dynamite didn't explode.

From the pulpit Martin warned his congregation that they would be facing very dangerous times but that under no circumstances should they retaliate with their own violence. The people listened to his words and heeded them. Finally, white city officials condemned the bombings and arrested those who were responsible. Things, it seemed, were starting to look up.

Together, Martin and Coretta became the face of the nonviolent civil rights movement. Martin was named president of the Southern Christian Leadership Conference (SCLC), which was headquartered in Atlanta, Georgia. The purpose of the conference was to spread the civil rights movement throughout the South.

Now Martin was so busy, he felt he had to resign his pastorship at the Dexter Avenue Baptist Church. The Kings moved to Atlanta, where Martin became a co-pastor under his father at the Ebenezer Baptist Church.

After reading Martin's book about the Montgomery bus boycott, *Stride Toward Freedom*, hundreds of Americans, many of them college students, eagerly joined the civil rights movement. They organized into the Student Nonviolent Coordinating Committee (SNCC). At Martin's urging, a training program was started to teach the students how to protest nonviolently. After each training session the students would sing hymns, but they soon began to change the words to fit the civil rights movement. One of the most popular songs was "We Shall Overcome." The students helped desegregate stores, swimming pools, and public restrooms. They were also involved in voter registration so black people would be able to vote for candidates they believed would represent their interests.

Stories about Coretta and Martin and their work in the civil rights movement appeared in leading magazines and newspapers, and on national television. At the request of the respective governments, Coretta and Martin traveled to Ghana and to India.

Back home, the Kings realized that the SCLC was running short of funds, so Coretta decided to tour the country, putting on what she called "freedom concerts." Martin was unsure about how much money, if any, could be raised that way, but once again, Coretta's faith in her musical ability allowed her to succeed, and the concerts added more than $50,000 to the Southern Christian Leadership Conference's treasury. Coretta was excited that she could use her musical talents to further the cause of civil rights.

Such world-wide attention made Coretta realize that she would have to control her famous temper, something she had seldom been able to do since she was a child. Now, with the world watching her and Martin's every move, she worked hard to choose both her friends and her words carefully. She didn't want anything that could be considered negative about her to detract from the importance of the movement.

In 1962 the Women's Strike for Peace held a meeting of its membership in Geneva, Switzerland. The organization was made up of women from around the world whose sole

192

purpose was to work together to give all children a better future. Coretta was invited to attend as a delegate from the United States. After the conference was over, Coretta was thoroughly convinced that if women everywhere united for peace, they would be a very powerful force.

Assassination

In 1963 Martin joined with the Reverend Fred Shuttlesworth to integrate Birmingham, Alabama. At that time, this was considered the most segregated city in the South. George Wallace, the governor of the state, lived by the slogan "Segregation Forever." He had never made any secret of the fact that he truly believed white people were better than black people. In fact, for many black Americans in Alabama, the living conditions were almost the same as they had been before the Civil War.

On May 2 the Children's Crusade, an organization of schoolchildren protesting the fact that they were made to attend substandard schools, began peacefully in Birmingham. The purpose was to draw attention to the deplorable conditions. On the second day of the march, though, Eugene "Bull" Conner, Birmingham's Public Safety Commissioner and a staunch advocate of racial segregation, attacked the marchers with vicious dogs, tear gas, and high-pressure water hoses. Almost one thousand children were arrested and taken into police custody.

Newspaper, magazine, and television reporters, sent to cover the event, were shocked, as were people in the rest of the United States and around the world. President John F. Kennedy even went on nationwide television to announce that he was sickened by what he had seen.

Coretta believed that the time had come for a major civil rights event that would show everyone just how terrible life was for black people—not only in the South, but in the rest of the country as well. She told Martin that they should take the movement to Washington, D.C. Coretta had no doubt that, if Martin asked them, all the other civil rights leaders would join with him in a march on the nation's capital.

On August 28, 1963, approximately 250,000 people, of all races, converged on the Mall, between the Lincoln Memorial and the Washington Monument, to demand an end to segregation. With Coretta seated behind him on the podium, Martin gave a speech that would become one of the most famous speeches in American history.

He told the huge crowd that he had had a dream where one day people of all races and religions would not be judged by the color of their skin but by their character, and that they would stand together free at last of prejudice. When Martin finished speaking, the crowd was silent at first, almost reverent, and then a tremendous roar went up. Coretta beamed. She knew in her heart that there was no stopping the movement now, that Martin's glorious dream would soon be fulfilled.

When President Kennedy proposed a bill that would grant equal rights to all races, Americans who were opposed to the idea reacted violently, and some of the civil rights workers lost their lives because of the struggle.

On Sunday, September 15, a bomb exploded at the Sixteenth Street Baptist Church in Birmingham, killing four young girls, and on November 22, President Kennedy was assassinated in Dallas.

The violence greatly disturbed Coretta and Martin. Several times over the years, Martin had tried to prepare Coretta for something similar happening to him, but she would tell him that she didn't believe it would happen. Now, her faith in that belief had been shaken to the core. It began to seem inevitable.

The new president, Lyndon Baines Johnson, from Texas, continued where President Kennedy had left off with the civil rights legislation. In 1964 both houses of Congress passed the Civil Rights Act.

That violent period ended with a peaceful event. Martin was awarded the Nobel Peace Prize. The entire family flew to Oslo, Norway, where Martin accepted the prize from the king of Norway.

In 1965 the Southern Christian Leadership Conference decided to begin registering black voters in Alabama. One of the first places they started was Coretta's hometown of Marion.

Even though everyone worked very hard, everything seem to conspire against the movement. It was as if whites who opposed equality for blacks had figured out every way possible to halt their efforts. Blacks would often stand in line for hours, waiting for the voter registration office to open only to be told that it was closed for the day. Similar events took place at voter registration offices all over the state. At the end of the SCLC's voting effort in Alabama, only thirty black people had been registered to vote, but almost four thousand protesters had been arrested. One protester had been killed, a young man by the name of Jimmy Lee Jackson. He was shot trying to protect some of his relatives who were also protesting.

Martin met with President Johnson on March 5, 1965, in an attempt to get him to pass the Voting Rights Act, which would guarantee every American, regardless of race, the right to cast his or her ballot in every election.

Martin remained in Washington, D.C., talking to members of both houses of Congress and other influential leaders in the capital, and he also began planning a march from Selma, Alabama, to Montgomery, the state capital, about fifty miles away. When George Wallace learned about the march, he immediately issued an order forbidding it. Martin decided that it should go ahead, anyway, on Sunday, March 7, and that Hosea Williams and John Lewis, two officials in the Southern Christian Leadership Conference, would lead it.

As the marchers crossed Selma's Edmund Pettus Bridge, waiting state troopers shouted to them that they had three minutes to stop, turn around, and return home or they would have to face the consequences. Some of the marchers, knowing what the troopers were capable of, did as they were told, but others knelt to pray.

Almost immediately, the state troopers, astride their horses, charged the kneeling marchers, swinging whips and clubs and firing canisters of tear gas. When it was over, seventy people had to be taken to the hospital, and fifty more were treated at the scene by stunned onlookers and television crews.

Once again, people around the world had seen racial violence in Alabama, and hundreds of civil rights volunteers descended on the state to protest the brutality.

Shortly afterward, James Reeb, a white minister from Boston, was killed by members of the Alabama Ku Klux Klan because he had come to the state to help African Americans in their struggle for equality. Afterward, protesters from all over the United States descended on the White House to demand that the Voting Rights Act be passed. President Johnson finally signed it into law on August 6, 1965.

For ten long years, the civil rights movement had been centered on the South, but both Coretta and Martin knew that racism also existed elsewhere in the United States, so they decided that the time had come to spread the movement to the north.

On January 22, 1966, the Kings moved to

Chicago. In order to share the daily struggles with the people they had come to help, they lived in an apartment in one of the city's poorest neighborhoods. Coretta was shocked by the conditions. The smell was horrible, there was almost no heat, and roaches were everywhere.

Right away the entire family went to work, helping tenants haul out piles of garbage, paint and plaster the walls, and sweep the stairwells free of dirt and litter. When they finished, the King family joined several thousand tenants in a march to protest the horrid living conditions in many of Chicago's black neighborhoods.

With Coretta and Martin's help, the Chicago branch of the Southern Christian Leadership Conference, led by the Reverend Jesse Jackson, organized Operation Breadbasket, the goal of which was to get better jobs and housing for all black people in the city.

• • •

The civil rights movement wasn't the only thing that concerned Coretta and Martin during this time, though. They were also against the war in Vietnam. When some of their friends in the movement told them that their negative comments about it would hurt the cause, Coretta calmly explained that you can't believe in peace at home if you don't believe in peace around the world.

By 1967 racial tensions had increased in the country. Some black Americans began to complain that Martin's nonviolent protests were not bringing about change fast enough. Some leaders felt that the majority of white Americans would only understand *violent* change and, instead of "Peace!" they began to chant, "Black power!" and "Burn, baby, burn!"

During the summer of 1967 riots and looting took place in several major American cities, and many people thought it was the beginning of a new civil war, but Coretta and Martin continued to insist that change, positive change, would only come about through slow, nonviolent methods, so they continued their work—now hated not only by some whites but by some black people as well.

In early 1968 members of the Sanitation Workers Union, in Memphis, Tennessee, most of whom were black, began to protest their poor wages and working conditions. When several of the men were beaten by the police during one of their marches, they contacted Martin, asking him if he would lead them. Martin agreed. On March 28 the workers, with Martin in front, had only traveled a few blocks when some of the younger members began breaking windows in nearby buildings and throwing rocks at the National Guard troops and the police, who attacked back.

Martin wasn't harmed, but he was disturbed that the rally had turned violent, something that went against all of his nonviolent teachings. Still, the union members pleaded with him to lead them on another march, and Martin agreed, but only after talking to them for more than an hour about how Gandhi succeeded in gaining India's independence with nonviolence. The march was scheduled for April 8.

On April 3 Martin joined with the workers for an evening rally, but he had received several death threats over the last few days, and he was in a very somber mood. In fact, when he spoke to the crowd, he told them he wasn't sure how much longer he would be living among them, but that he didn't fear death, and they shouldn't either, as they continued to struggle for rights that had been denied them too long. The audience stood and cheered.

On the evening of April 4, as Martin was standing on a balcony of the Lorraine Motel, in Memphis, James Earl Ray aimed a rifle at him and pulled the trigger.

Coretta Keeps Martin's Dream Alive

People all around the world were shocked and saddened by Martin's assassination. While some expressed their grief by sending Coretta thousands of telegrams and letters, others reacted violently, and there were riots in more than one hundred cities across the United States.

Coretta was also overwhelmed by visitors to their house in Atlanta. She greeted as many guests as she could, took care of the funeral arrangements, and tried to keep up the spirits of their children. Throughout it all, Coretta retained her dignity.

The day before Martin's funeral, Coretta and her children marched at the head of the Sanitation Workers Union's protest in Memphis, Tennessee. When people questioned her about it, she told them in no uncertain terms that she believed Martin would have wanted her to do it.

Martin's funeral was held on April 9. Afterward, more than 150,000 mourners marched behind the mule-drawn wagon carrying his casket to the South View Cemetery in Atlanta.

The next morning, early, Coretta began her life without Martin.

One of her first projects was to fulfill Martin's work by building The Martin Luther King Jr. Center for Nonviolent Social Change. Although years of planning, fund-raising, and lobbying for the center lay ahead, Coretta made sure she also stayed involved in all the civil rights causes that had been so dear to Martin's heart.

Coretta's autobiography, *My Life with Martin Luther King Jr.*, was published in 1969. She revised it in 1993.

As the decade of the 1970s began, Coretta continued Martin's commitment to economic justice for all Americans. In 1974 she formed and served as cochair of the Full Employment Action Council. This coalition of more than one hundred religious, labor, business, civil rights, and women's rights organizations dedicated itself to making sure every American was not only fully employed but could take advantage of all the economic opportunities the country offered.

The King Center finally opened in Atlanta in 1981. It is housed in the Freedom Hall complex, which was constructed around Martin's tomb, and is the first ever center of its kind built in the memory of a black American leader. Its library and archives house the largest collection of civil rights era documents in the nation. More than one million people a year visit this national historic site.

Throughout the rest of the decade of the 1980s Coretta continued her civil rights work with goodwill missions to Africa, Central and South America, Europe, and Asia.

In 1983 to celebrate the twentieth anniversary of the historic March on Washington, Coretta led a gathering of more than eight hundred human rights organizations in the largest such demonstration the city had seen since 1963.

Coretta also led the successful campaign to establish Martin's birthday, January 15, as a national holiday. By an Act of Congress, the first observance took place in 1986. Today, Martin's birthday is celebrated in more than one hundred other countries.

In September 1993 Coretta was invited to the

White House by President Bill Clinton to witness the historic handshake between the leaders of Israel and the Palestine Liberation Organization at the Middle East Peace Accords.

Coretta stood next to Nelson Mandela when he was sworn in as the president of the Republic of South Africa in 1994. Ten years earlier, Coretta and her children had been arrested in front of the South African Embassy in Washington, D.C., for protesting against the then white regime's policy of racial separation, known as apartheid.

In 2004 Coretta returned to Antioch College to celebrate its 150th anniversary. She was presented with the prestigious Horace Mann Award.

Coretta suffered a stroke in August of 2005, which left her partially paralyzed and unable to speak. That November, though, when Edythe celebrated her eightieth birthday, Coretta managed to sing "Happy Birthday" to her over the telephone.

On January 14, 2006, Coretta made her first public appearance since her stroke, at a Salute to Greatness dinner in honor of Martin. She rose from her wheelchair, leaned on her children, and waved to the crowd. The people cheered her for a long time.

Two weeks later, on January 30, 2006, Coretta died at a sanatorium in Mexico's Baja peninsula. Newspapers and television stations around the world informed millions of listeners that the voice that had inspired millions of disenfranchised people all over the world to speak out for justice had been silenced. What Coretta and Martin accomplished together through their work in the civil rights movement, though, will continue forever.

For More Information

BOOKS

King, Coretta Scott. *My Life with Martin Luther King, Jr.* (Revised Edition). New York: Penguin Books USA, Inc., 1993.

McPherson, Stephanie Sammartino. *Coretta Scott King.* Minneapolis: Twenty-First Century Books.

Vivian, Octavia. *Coretta, The Story of Coretta Scott King* (Commemorative Edition). Minneapolis: Fortress Press, 2006.

Waxman, Laura Hamilton. *Coretta Scott King.* Minneapolis: Lerner Publications Company, 2008.

WEBSITES

The Martin Luther King Jr. Center for
Nonviolent Social Change:
http://www.thekingcenter.org

Coretta Scott and Martin Luther King Jr.
information:
http://www.stanford.edu/group/King/about_King/
details/27042b.htm